M000013308

Copyright © 2021 by Mari Dietz

All rights reserved.

No part of this book may be reproduced in any form or by any electronic or mechanical means, including information storage and retrieval systems, without written permission from the author, except for the use of brief quotations in a book review.

 Created with Vellum

MAGIC'S CURSE

Founders Series Book Three

MARI DIETZ

To all the strong women in my life,
You give me the courage to speak out when I'm afraid, and
I know you will always have my back.
You are the reason I hope to continue to write strong
female characters.
Keep fighting.

Vic glared at the gray stone arches in front of her while waiting in the Verrin town square. The main canal bubbled to her right and carried the chatter of people going to work at GicCorp. Stone walls dominated one side of the square, with a letter marking each entrance. In the northeast corner, the domed building of the founders' government didn't reach as high as the corporation, a testament to who really controlled the city. The founders were gathering today to vote out the Nordics. Less than a week had gone by since the battle at Haven, and the founders insisted they could win the vote. The founders needed to agree on which family would take the Nordics' place, which had caused many arguments in her father's office. Too many people wanted the power, and Vic worried nothing would change.

The humid air made her black clothing stick to her body. The stone wall she leaned against provided some coolness to her back. Her stomach grumbled at the smoky smell of alligator and beef coming from the nearby restaurant. The rebellion felt untouchable, but Vic knew that was a delusion. The Nordics wouldn't go down with just a vote.

Kai leaned on the stone wall next to her, his brown eyes fixed on the arches as well. His russet curls were tied back off his neck, but he didn't have the decency to sweat while they waited.

"How long does the vote take?" His words ruined his appearance of calm. Kai crossed his arms and ignored the townspeople's glances. For all they knew, it was a normal day and the Verrin government functioned as usual. The reapers being out this early in the morning was the only odd occurrence.

A scream pierced the air. A founder ran out of the building, clutching his neck. Vic pushed off the wall, leaped up the stairs, and caught the founder's falling body.

"We need a healer!" Vic faced forward, hoping someone in the square would listen.

A rush of people ran off, hopefully to find a healer.

The Silver founder grasped her arm, leaving a bloody stain on her black clothing, and gurgled, "Run."

His eyes rolled back, and his movements stilled. Blood pooled around him as Vic gently placed him on the stone ground. He'd been one of their allies.

Vic grasped her scythe from its harness. Running into the building, she flicked it open in one movement, Kai tight on her heels. The founder had never said which direction she should run.

A chilly breeze carried the smell of blood as she burst through the large wooden door into the chamber that only founders were allowed in during their sessions. The chamber was round and wide under a stone domed ceiling. Natural light came through the many windows built into the dome. They stood on the second-floor balcony that encircled the room. Wooden doors lined the space, but Vic didn't know where they led.

Black-clad bodies in masks wielded scythes against the founders below. Chairs were overturned, and roots from various trees burst through the ground, wrapping around the masked attackers. Metal spikes speared some in a gruesome display. The founders fought with their magic, but their bodies also littered the floor. It couldn't be real reapers they fought. Vic scanned the room for her father. If they were killing rebel allies, they would target him.

A hand yanked her out of the way as metal spikes jutted from the wall. The Steel founder's lips twisted in a snarl, his wand glowing. He was using the metal from the door hinges to try to spear them. Kai had pulled her out of the way in time.

Vic swallowed and ran around the wide, circular room. "We're the enemy. They're using people dressed like reapers."

Kai's jaw tightened. "It appears that way."

Imposter bodies lay strewn across the chamber, their blood soaking into the thick rug. The founder imbs could pack a magical punch, but since the imposters weren't using magic, they could fight until the founders' wands ran out. It took too much magic to manipulate materials in combat.

Running around the balcony, Vic finally spotted her father across the room.

His copper hair glowed under the lights, and he threw black sand in the air. As it fell, he turned it into glass shards that speared his victim.

"Remind me never to mess with your dad."

"Same." She shivered at her father's calm composure as

he shredded people alive. She'd never seen him battle in a real-life situation before. She was happy he was on their side.

They stayed behind a pillar, knowing they would have enemies on both sides if they joined the fray.

Her father saw her, and fear flashed in his face. He waved his hand and mouthed at them to run. Vic wasn't used to seeing him without his metaphorical founder's mask in place. If her father was afraid, it meant they were losing.

Kai pulled her behind a pillar. "It feels wrong not to help them." He met her eyes. "Should we leave?"

As reapers, they fought monsters nightly, with little time for fear. She looked desperately at her battling father, who kept glancing their way. "If we stay, we'll make it worse." Her body rebelled at the thought, but they could knock out some imposters on their way out.

They flicked their scythes closed but held them steady. Founders and imposters battled by the exits. The steel pikes remained unmovable, and no one could get out that way. They would have to cross to the other side.

Kai bent low and ran forward as she kept pace behind him. The Grain founder in the middle wove thick stalks of wheat around an imposter. It looked like the founders had gained the upper hand, but she had a feeling that most of the dead founders had tried to vote out the Nordics. So much for winning the diplomatic way.

A stone wall burst across their path, and Kai rammed straight into it. They turned, but another stone wall was behind them.

The Stone founder stalked toward them, his jowls shaking in triumph. He'd left a window in the wall and peeped at them with his beady eyes.

"My my, it's the disgraced Glass daughter. You can't kill us all." He tapped his wand against the stone.

"You're framing the reapers?"

Stone didn't answer, but the walls moved in on them to make a reaper sandwich.

The only way out was to jump down into the main battle.

Vic reached for Kai. "It isn't a day out with me unless we jump at least once."

Despite the battle, Kai snorted, and holding each other's hands, they jumped down to the main floor. They let go to tuck and roll. The leap jarred her bones, but nothing broke. The carpet squelched under their feet with blood. Vic made a beeline for the open exit, knowing she didn't need to wait for Kai.

Blood smeared the chairs, and Tristan fought at the head of the stage. His brown hair was perfect, and he seemed in no rush to kill the imposter fighting him. His opponent's jerky movements gave it away: they weren't trained fighters.

"Blight, they're killing radiant dressed as reapers." The poor souls had been forced into labor, and now they were fodder for Tristan's plot. GicCorp had ordered the radiant to attack, only to kill them off.

Pity narrowed Kai's eyes. "Keep going. We can't do anything now."

Some founders noticed Vic, and their expressions soured. In their minds, her presence confirmed that the reapers were there to kill them. They'd fallen right into Tristan's web.

The chair next to Vic stretched out to wrap around her. She dove and rolled on the blood-soaked rugs. Her hair clung to her neck from a mixture of sweat and now someone else's blood.

Vic held in her disgust. Kai flicked open his scythe and culled the branches the Timber founder created.

"Watch it!" Vic pushed Kai out of the way of a metal spear. The point scraped her side, but she would be fine.

The door loomed ahead, and they ran through. A wall of glass shimmered across the doorway behind them, blocking them from entering the building and others from following them. Vic silently thanked her father.

"Where to?"

"Back to my house. We need to get the other reapers out." Vic sprinted, scythe in hand. How many houses could they warn? Or were they too late?

Kai tugged her toward an express water taxi, and she hopped in. It would be faster than running.

"Eastside Dock!" Kai looked behind them to see if anyone followed.

The driver nodded and took off. Vic sat on the edge of the water taxi all the way to the dock and leaped out the instant the taxi docked.

The Glass house shone in the morning light. Vic slammed the doors open, and something shattered on the ground.

"Evacuate to the base!" Kai swiftly ran up the stairs.

The people in the house leaped into action. Reapers packed their belongings, and it looked like no one had even slept there.

William approached, with Samuel behind him. His pack was on his back, and he held her cat, Scraps, in his arms. His blue eyes examined her. "Are you bleeding?"

Vic grimaced and pulled the sticky shirt away from her body. "It's not all mine." Her heart fluttered at his concern, but she pushed the feeling aside. Nothing could ever happen. Her skin itched where her orb used to be. Her life was ticking down.

William seemed to be having an inner debate. "We're headed out. Are you coming too?"

Vic and Kai's job in the evacuation was to make sure everyone made it out first. She wanted to see if her father was okay before she ran off. "I'll meet you down at Base One." Only a week ago, she'd joked about living in the sewers. Maybe she should have kept her mouth shut.

He nodded and left with Samuel. She was glad he hadn't insisted on staying and would be safe.

In the week before the vote, they'd made an evacuation plan with the founders and reapers. The founders hadn't thought it would be needed, but their democracy had failed within minutes. The reapers who hadn't brought their families to the founders' homes would need to get them, as GicCorp might go after them. The rebellion had tried to plan for everything. They would need the imbs and their wands for healing and to grow food at the base, but they only trusted the reapers' families.

The reapers spaced out their departure from the Glass house. Vic watched from the window as they all went in different directions. None of the reapers wore black, and their scythes stayed stashed away to avoid detection. Their brands would be a problem, though. In the middle of summer, who wore scarves or high collars? If someone knew what to look for, the reapers would stick out.

The house quieted down, and Vic did a round to check all the rooms. Her sister sat on her bed with a pack on her back. Her room still looked like a rainbow had thrown up in it.

Emilia rushed to her. "You're injured?"

Vic smiled. "Only a little. Where do you think you're going with that pack?"

Emilia crossed her arms. "I'm going with you."

Vic would feel at ease if she could have her sister with her, but Emilia would be safer with their father. "Not a chance. We went through this when you were eavesdropping on our plans." When their father had found out that Em was listening in, he'd restricted her to her room, something he hadn't done since they were little. Vic thought his reaction had been extreme, but she trusted him to keep her safe.

"I'm an adult, and I get to decide." Emilia adjusted the straps on her shoulders. "I'm supposed to be in Haven, so I'm in as much danger as you are. All I do is stay in my room all day. I'm going mad."

Vic wanted to hug her but kept her distance to prevent blood from getting on her sister. "It won't be any different where we're going. Do you think you'll get to wander around? You'll likely be stuck in a dark room."

The stubborn tilt in her sister's face didn't disappear, and a weird desperation filled her eyes. She was probably worried that Tristan would find her.

"Remember, you're coming later with Mom and Dad. Just wait."

Before Emilia could argue, their mother appeared, out of breath. "Vic, come with me. Emilia, stay in your room." Their mother tugged on Vic. Her usually neat golden hair stuck out in places from the rush of getting people out of the house.

Vic followed her mother down the glass stairs and to her father's office. Her mother opened the hidden room behind her father's desk and gestured for Vic to go inside. She handed Vic a pack. "I saw you running around in bloody clothing. Hurry. You too, Kai."

Vic hadn't even seen Kai, and she jumped.

"On edge, Sparks?" Kai joined her in the room.

"Stay in here until we hear from your father."

Vic eyed the room that housed their family's relics. "Why can't we go?"

"They know you. It's better to wait." The door shut with a whoosh.

Vic sighed. At least they weren't sitting together in the dark. Since Kai had taken over the Order, they'd been on delicate ground. He'd gone from someone Vic had thought she could care about romantically to a tentative friend after their raid on Haven. Thoughts of William crossed her mind as she stood alone with Kai.

The wands on the shelves radiated their own light. Kai's lips pressed into a straight line as he took in the wealth of a Founder family.

"I know it's not fair," Vic said as she rummaged through the pack. Her mother had even put in a damp towel on top.

Kai politely turned his back while she cleaned off the blood as best she could. "I didn't say anything."

Vic peeled off her shirt, quickly swiped her body, and put on a clean green shirt. She frowned at the color. After wearing black for so long, it was strange. The color made her feel like a blinking target.

"You didn't have to. I know what the city goes through too. Maybe we can actually change it."

Kai touched a first-generation relic but jerked his hand back as if it had shocked him. "I'd like to hope so, but I think our only chance is to leave these walls."

Vic froze before changing into her pants. "Leave?" She could read nothing from his solid back.

"Leave."

She finished changing and pulled on his arm. "How can we get out before we turn into mogs? The records—"

"I know we have these journals that tell us people died trying to get out of the swamp." His face softened. "But what if that's another lie GicCorp is telling us to keep us here? Maybe a pack of reapers could get out and see what's beyond the swamp."

"What if it's just more swamp?"

"Then we'll know."

"We can't sacrifice people on a hunch." Vic shoved her bloody clothes into the pack and hissed when she stretched her wound.

Kai took the pack from her hands. "You didn't wrap it."

Vic waved him off. "It's small."

"Sit."

She plopped onto the floor. "It's suicide going outside the wall."

Kai's fingers brushed against her skin as he lifted the bottom of her shirt. He clicked his tongue. "You got blood on this now."

She rested her hand on his wrist. "Please, don't do this."

His eyes warmed as he gently removed her hand and cleaned her wound. "I'm not the one who'd be going."

"Who?"

"Ivy and Freddie will lead the team."

The air left her lungs. "Why?" The minute she got down to the hidden base, she would talk to them. This was an insane mission.

"They brought the idea first."

From the pack, Kai pulled out the bandage Vic had ignored and placed it over her cut. He patted it a few times and ran his hand over the creases.

Vic's emotions swarmed in her head, but in the dark room, her world shrank as Kai traced the bandage before finally dropping her shirt.

"You're very thorough." Vic willed her body to cool down.

His full lips smiled. "That I am."

When had it gotten so hot in here?

Vic started at the sound of a door slamming in her house.

"I don't appreciate you following me home. I need to make sure my wife is safe." Vic could hear her father's icy voice on the other side of the door.

"I'm sure she's safe," Tristan replied. "Now you both need to turn in your wands."

Kai stilled. They leaned into the door, listening in on the conversation.

"I don't know what you're going on about."

Something thudded in the room. "Your daughter was seen with the reapers. The remaining founders voted to rid Verrin of all reapers." Vic held in a gasp. "If you are sheltering your daughter, you're waiving your rights to a relic, unless you disown her."

A long pause came from her father's office. Vic clenched her hands. Her father had warned her that this might happen in the coming days, but her heart still hurt.

"Fine, I will officially disown her in front of witnesses. Is this really of so much importance that you would leave the scene of a massacre?"

"Oh, my old, old friend. It really is."

Something crashed, and Vic grabbed the handle, but Kai stopped her.

Tristan continued to talk, but his voice was more muffled. "Our deal is off."

"It was off the moment you broke your word about my daughter."

Vic met Kai's eyes, and he looked as surprised as she did. What deal was he talking about? Was it about her or Emilia?

"Be seeing you, *Conrad*."

Silence came from the other side of the door, and Vic and Kai remained frozen. They pressed against the wall, his hand holding her wrist.

The door slid open, and they stumbled away. Her father stood at the entrance, clutching his left forearm.

"Are you hurt, Father?"

He waved her off. "You need to leave. There may not be another chance to get to the hideout."

Vic hadn't been to the underground base. Apparently, that was what her father had been filling his days with down in the sewers. When she'd questioned him about the need for a secret base, he'd brushed her off, saying, "It only matters that we have it. It took a long time to prepare something that the other founders wouldn't find."

Her father placed a hand on Kai's shoulder. "Look after my daughter."

"I will."

Vic didn't look away from the arm her father had been cradling. "I'm more than capable of looking after myself."

Her father's face softened. "That you are."

"Keep Em and Mother safe." Vic didn't want to leave them behind, but it was for the best. How long would they have to stay underground? She was more of a danger to them anyway. She wasn't infected with blight yet, but it was only a matter of time. Then she would have to choose between getting help from Kai or William, and she already knew who she would choose. Until that day arrived, she would fight GicCorp.

"Get going, you two." Her father brushed a strand of hair away from her face. "Stay alive."

Vic and Kai ran out of the house. Her father's expression stayed with her as they made it over the wall. The nearest entrance to a sewer was in the middle of the street. Most people didn't go down into the sewers during the day, unless they were imbs working.

Kai kept watch as they moved the grate. The steamy sewers made Vic want to vomit, but she jumped into the darkness below ground. Kai followed shortly after.

"This way."

They put on their masks and ran in the fading light of the tunnels. Vic didn't know when she would get to see daylight again, but she kept running since that was all she knew.

The heat wasn't as overwhelming in the sewers, but it didn't help the smell. Kai veered away from the major lines and the reaper paths. They needed to watch out for dips in the crumbling pathway and the occasional rat. A clean-smelling breeze startled Vic as they wove deeper into the depths of the city. Kai took off his mask and stopped. Vic almost ran into his back.

"The ventilation is better here, away from the main lines. I don't know how your father did it, but the smell isn't as overwhelming."

Vic copied him and removed her mask. The breeze on her sweaty face was refreshing. The tunnel didn't feel so confining.

They approached a section of rock, and Vic squinted. The hidden door reflected the light slightly more than the surrounding stone. The hidden glass door wasn't noticeable unless you looked for it.

"Your father said you can only see out of the glass." Kai approached and showed his neck brand to the wall.

After a while, Vic thought Kai might be in the wrong spot, but the rocky-looking glass rolled to the side, the pieces melding like they were nothing.

A young woman with bright eyes and a careful smile nodded to them. "Welcome to Base One. I'm Janesa." She was tall, with her hair pulled back into a low bun. A bright blue stone glowed at the end of her wand. "Your father put me in charge of this entrance. Many people are already here and waiting in the main area."

"Thanks, Janesa." Kai walked past her, and when Vic crossed over, the glass scraped shut behind them with a crunch.

To the left of the tunnel was a room carved out of stone. Looking back at the glass entryway, Vic could see the tunnel clearly. It was eerie to think that no one could see them. If someone wasn't paying attention, they could run into the wall. It would give the imb guarding it a good laugh.

The air was even cleaner in these tunnels. They zig-zagged for a span, then the tunnel opened into a large space of smooth black rock that curved upward. Vic paused. It looked like the area where she'd found the dull stones and piles of junk, only this place didn't have a smelly sewage river. Rows of pathways circled down the walls. Stairs connected all the levels, and hundreds of doors dotted the dome. On the ground level, many people sat in the center of the smooth black floor and on glass benches, chatting in whispers. The reapers stood protectively around the edges. Vic wondered how many glass entrances there were, and if her father trusted all the imbs he'd chosen.

"Let's get our room assignments."

They walked down the circular path, and on closer inspection, Vic saw it was made of glass. How long had it taken her father to build this? The rooms they passed also had numbered glass doors. Vic assumed the occupants could see out. It took longer to make one-way glass. He must have suspected something from the very beginning.

Vic breathed a sigh of relief when she saw Bomrosy, William, and Samuel. Xiona trailed behind Bomrosy.

Bomrosy hugged her. "Glad you made it." Her long braids were tied back, away from her face, and a pack hung off her back. "We got most of my tools out before the evacuation."

"Did anyone not make it?"

"They're checking now."

All the reapers had hoped they wouldn't need this plan when her father had brought it up to the commanders, but with everyone in one location, maybe they would come up with a better plan of attack.

"I don't think anyone anticipated that Tristan would dress his radiant army up like reapers and attack the founders." Bomrosy let someone go ahead of her as she talked with them. William flinched at Bomrosy's revelation.

William had followed the radiant path, believing in the calling until he'd found out his father had purified people by force. The foundation of the radiant life was that people were supposed to choose this path of their own free will. William had changed so much since Vic had first met him, and he'd become someone she relied on and cared about as maybe more than a friend. Standing between Kai and William, though, she felt awkward. One was fire and the other a steady wind, but together they might explode.

"Did you get your room assignments?" Kai asked.

"I'm in the workshop with Xiona," Bomrosy answered. "Your family's over there. They want four to five in a room, but there are smaller accommodations near the meeting room for commanders."

Bomrosy pointed to the second floor. There was one wider door in the middle, flanked by doors that were closer together. Vic found Kai's family, and his sister had already found other kids to play with, their parents watching them with smiles. The children made it feel almost normal to live underground.

"They're putting those with young children at the top, closest to the escape routes," Bomrosy added.

Vic could tell Kai was debating whether to stay close to his family or the other leaders.

"We can look out for your mother and sister," William offered. Scraps pawed at his sleeves, and he let him down. The kids squealed and petted the cat while Scraps purred like a king.

Kai motioned to the table. "Let's go see which rooms are left first."

An imb sat with a list and looked up as they approached. He shoved his glasses up on his nose. "Name and how many in your party?"

This person made it feel like they were staying in a hotel.

"Kai. I'm the commander of Nyx."

The imb looked down at his list and passed Kai two keys. "Your family is on the top floor, and we placed you on the second."

"Who's near my family?"

"Other families with children. However, your family is above the workshop like the Glass founder requested. Their room is smaller, but they're the only ones in it for now."

Kai nodded.

"Xiona and I are near your family, so we can check on them often," Bomrosy said.

"I'd appreciate it."

Vic stepped up. "Victoria Glass."

The imb looked at his list. "You don't have an assignment. Is there anyone you would like to stay with? The notes your father gave us mention that you will be part of the meetings, so you may want a single room."

"I don't mind staying with others." Vic wasn't a commander, and she didn't want special treatment just because her father had built this. She was the same as everyone else now. She also wanted someone to monitor her for blight infection.

"She can stay with my brother and me."

"And you are?" the imb asked.

"William and Sam."

The imb wrote down their names. "Here's a four-person room on the second floor."

Kai's hand shot out to stop him from giving them the keys. "Vic, you don't need to stay with them. You might be more comfortable in your own space."

Vic shrugged and reached past him. "I don't mind sharing. I'm not a commander. They can give those rooms to those who need it."

"I don't think you'll be comfortable with two strange men."

Vic laughed. "Strange men? Kai, they're my friends."

William took the key from the imb and asked, "What are you afraid will happen, Kai?"

Glaring at William, Kai didn't move his arm. "Your father would be more comfortable if you stayed with Bomrosy."

Vic pushed his arm back. "I'm okay. Thanks for your

strange concern about my dangerous living situation with two brothers who've never harmed me." Vic pocketed the glass key. She didn't understand the expression on Kai's face as he looked between her and William.

"Fine. I would prefer if you didn't stay with him."

Kai's stance widened, and William pulled at his cuffs. They turned, and their gazes landed on Vic. She was tired of Kai's attitude. She didn't need his permission on where to stay.

Before Vic could speak, Bomrosy cut in, "O-kay, then." Bomrosy pushed them away from the table to the side of the room. "I'll be in my workshop. Vic, you are more than welcome to stay with me, but I'll leave you and your boyfriends to decide where you're staying."

"They aren't my boyfriends!"

Bomrosy waved as she walked to the stairs that led up to her place.

Kai and William gave her expectant looks. Kai's arms crossed over his muscular chest, and William put his hands in his pockets, his blue eyes piercing her.

"I'm not sure this is the time or place to talk about this." Vic sighed. "I'll just stay with Bomrosy. I'm tired, and I don't want to get in the middle of something."

Vic adjusted her pack and went after Bomrosy. She'd just witnessed a bloodbath and couldn't think about Kai and William. Untangling her feelings about them would have to wait. She'd thought she and Kai were friends, but he obviously didn't want her with someone else. She couldn't help her disappointment that she wouldn't be around William. While looking for her sister, she'd found his presence peaceful. He'd become her steady wind in the storm. The nights she'd fallen asleep in his arms, she'd felt the safest and the rage inside her had calmed.

The glass key pressed against her leg in her pocket. She could stop by and see him. Vic climbed the steps to the third floor and entered the room. It already had the familiar Bomrosy workroom smell of oil and dust. Xiona and Bomrosy had stacked crates of tools, and they worked quietly to hang them up.

Vic set down her pack. "What's the big project that got you this space?"

Bomrosy snorted. "I knew you would chicken out."

"What?"

Bomrosy placed another tool on the wall and faced her friend. "I knew you couldn't let one of them down easy."

Vic rifled through her bag, pulled out a hair tie, and put her long red hair up in a bun. "Whatever do you mean?" Her voice sounded a bit high-pitched.

"Sure."

Bomrosy took out a pouch with a few rings inside. "To answer your question, they asked me to find out about radiant magic. William and I are going to work together."

"To see if you can reverse it? How'll that go, working with him?" Bomrosy didn't care much for William since he'd forcibly cleansed Xiona to save them.

Bomrosy arranged the rings on the table. "There isn't much to go on. This magic works differently and has never really been studied. It isn't like they had volunteers to become radiant to test. Now we have Xiona and Sam."

Vic eyed the rings. "Where did you get those?"

"I made them. I don't know if they work. Like I said, no one's going to test them, and I don't really want to test them on anyone. We only have William's ring to work with, and if something happens to it, we might be in trouble." Bomrosy held up a ring. "So many people died today because they were forced to fight. We want to undo their purification."

"If anyone can do it, you can."

"Thanks for the vote of confidence. I'm worried we may never figure out how to undo it." Bomrosy's face fell as she watched Xiona hang up her tools. "If I succeed, Xiona will end up in jail."

Vic sat next to her friend. "But she would be in control of her own thoughts again. She might already be in jail now."

"You're right. I'm not saying I won't try hard to reverse it, but it seems like I'm always in a no-win situation."

"I understand that completely."

They spent the rest of the time organizing Bomrosy's workshop. After a while, the exhaustion of the day caught up to Vic, and Bomrosy insisted she go shower and get some sleep.

The bathrooms were communal, and the water pressure wasn't great, but Vic was happy to wash away the day and put on another set of clean clothing. She took out her dirty clothes, including the blood-soaked black reaper clothing, and washed them as well. She rewrapped the cut on her side.

When she got back to the workshop, Kai was sitting on a bench, setting out food. He tentatively looked at Vic. "I grabbed your dishes for you."

"Thanks." Why was he acting so awkward? Vic went to hang her wet clothes on a line in the workshop as Kai dished out soup and cut a loaf of bread.

"Are the founders getting us these supplies?" Vic asked.

"Yes. We don't know how long this will last. Reports are coming in from above that things are in chaos. Reapers are to be arrested on sight. Any founders discovered with reapers will also be in danger. And there's a strict curfew. Everyone needs to be inside by nightfall." He dug into his soup. "We have imbs setting up in an area to grow food, but it won't be easy providing for everyone."

Vic shook her head and ate the food. It felt like ages since she'd eaten. "How's Tristan dealing with the mog situation?"

"Apparently, he's promising a new way to deal with mogs."

"Oh, because he can control them?" She wondered how the imbs or the freelance reapers felt above ground. Would the imbs accept Tristan's new rule? What choice did they have when GicCorp controlled the charging stations?

Kai laughed. "Something like that."

Bomrosy sat down and handed a bowl to Xiona. "How does he control them?"

"We don't know."

Vic's neck itched. There was something about the gicorb and Tristan's power. No one knew she was living on borrowed time. "It has something to do with the orbs."

Bomrosy stopped eating. "What makes you say that?"

"I didn't want to tell you all so soon." Vic touched her neck. "But I no longer have a gicorb."

Kai pushed back from the table, rattling the dishes. "And when were you going to mention that tidbit?"

"I should have said something sooner, but I don't want everyone looking at me like I'm about to die." They stared at her. "Yes, like that."

"What are we going to do? We have to get you a new one!" Kai got up from the table, and Vic grabbed his hand to pull him back down.

"We know that's impossible." Vic's throat was thick as she swallowed. "When I was fighting Tristan, I felt him controlling me. The feeling came from the orb. If he can control us through the orb, maybe that's how he can control the mogs."

Bomrosy froze. "What if it's the same for the radiants?"

Vic shook her head. "They don't have orbs."

Bomrosy stirred her soup with a vacant expression. "Yes. Sorry, I just ... but this can also mean something too." She remained lost in her thoughts.

This was how Bomrosy worked, and maybe she would make some connection. Vic turned her attention back to Kai, who'd sat back down but wasn't eating. Her situation felt more real now that she'd said it out loud. "With the battle and the plans to evacuate, I didn't have to think about my future. I just accepted that it was over."

Vic didn't want to die, but there wasn't much they could do.

"We can keep draining you."

"You know that isn't a permanent solution."

Kai took her hand and clenched it. "Maybe it will work until we can find one."

Vic didn't know what else to tell him. He might need to end things for her before or after she became a mog.

"Would you ever think to ask William—"

"You know I won't." Vic focused on her food. The thought of being a mindless puppet scared her more than death. Now with Tristan and his army of radiant, she feared that option even more. Vic had lost her appetite. "Kai."

"Yes?"

"I'm not asking to be saved, but please let me be a part of

everything. And don't tell anyone else. I need to stay busy. I can't sit here, thinking about it."

The only one who continued to eat was Xiona, and her spoon scraping her dish became louder in the silence.

"I can keep an eye on her at night," Bomrosy said softly. Her understanding eyes made Vic thankful.

"I'm meeting with the other captains and seconds to decide on a plan tonight," Kai said. "If you don't want to mention this to anyone else, it would be best that you work with me." He got up again and went to the door. "You ask so much, Sparks. Too much, sometimes." He left the room and shut the door firmly behind him.

Bomrosy gathered the dishes. "What does he mean?"

"He knows he'll have to be the one to kill me."

V ic stretched out as she got up from the stone floor. There hadn't been a chance to bring down bedding, so everyone made do with what they'd brought. Over time, maybe they could bring down more items, but the priority was food. Cots would be made by hand to preserve the imbs' power for healing and growing food. The lamps were on their lowest setting, and it was hard to see without sunlight.

Bomrosy had stayed up late working on something and still slept. Vic appreciated that Bomrosy hadn't forced her talk last night. Putting her gicorb out of her mind was for the best right now. Her eyes remained normal, and Kai would drain her for as long as he could, but until it was over, she would help.

They'd sent out a notice last night that the reapers would meet early in the morning, likely to get assignments. Everyone knew they wouldn't be safe forever; GicCorp would find them eventually. Verrin was large, but the rebels would run out of places to hide. People also needed to charge, which might become a problem with credits.

Vic got ready as quietly as possible, and after a visit to the bathroom, she went down to the bottom of the base where the other reapers gathered. The commanders were already waiting for them. She nodded to Landon. Following the attack at Haven, they'd come to an understanding. He would never be on her friend list, but his crude comments had stopped. Kai kept Landon close because the Nyx reapers were still wary of him, although Landon had never demanded that Kai step down.

Across the room, Ivy sat with Freddie. Before Vic could make her way to them, the commanders called for silence. Vic sat down with a frustrated sigh. She wanted to work things out with Ivy and Freddie but hadn't had the chance. If they went over the wall, she might never see them again.

Becks stepped to the center of the commanders and their seconds. She commanded attention with her muscular frame. Her copper eyes focused on anyone who dared to talk, and Vic remembered that glare well.

"We're all in the same situation now. The other commanders and I agree that to survive, we need to work together."

A young woman, who Vic assumed was Becks's second, stepped forward and handed her papers.

Becks took them from her. "We're going to assign tasks and figure out a way to fight the Nordics and the other founders. Right now, we're mostly spying, but we'll keep everyone informed. If you have any ideas, share them to your commanders and seconds." Becks held out the papers. "Sign up for a task and we'll go from there."

Vic wondered which one Kai wanted her on so he could keep an eye on her.

"One group will keep hunting mogs in the sewers. We need to keep collecting blight to charge. The second group will stake out Haven and try to capture radiant. Our citizens are being used against their will, and I, for one, don't want to harm them. The last group will have the most dangerous mission." Becks paused, and Vic knew what was coming. "A group wants to go out into the swamps to see if there is anything beyond."

Gasps came from the crowd. Vic gripped her knees and stole a glance at Ivy.

"It will be dangerous, we're just waiting for capture. We might need a way out of Verrin, if there is one. I do ask that you don't sign up if you have any family."

The swamp task sounded like a suicide mission. Maybe she should talk to Kai and go with the reapers. If she was going to die soon, she might as well help them fight mogs.

As if he'd heard her thoughts, their eyes met, and he shook his head.

Vic tilted her head in response, and he stared her down.

"Speak to your commanders and figure out where they want to place you. We'll make the schedule tonight. This isn't a perfect situation, but the important thing is that we're alive."

Becks went back to stand with the other commanders. The crowd of reapers hesitated, maybe wondering if they should clap, but after a while, they went up to their commanders.

Vic looked for Ivy and Freddie, but they'd already disappeared. She didn't know when they would leave, but they couldn't hide from her for long. She waited while Kai and Landon assigned tasks to their reapers.

Kai signaled her over, and he stepped off to the side. "I'll sign you up to collect radiant with me."

"Fun."

"I know what you're thinking." He handed her a paper and a pencil.

Vic took them from him. "Oh? What am I thinking?"

"You want to go on that crazy mission." He'd kept his voice low, but Vic still looked to see if anyone had heard him.

"So you agree it's a suicide mission?" The paper he'd handed her said "Haven," and there was a signature line at the bottom. "Since I'm a ticking time bomb, why not go?" She would hate to say her goodbyes early, but it might be better while she still had control of her mind.

Kai pushed her hand that held the pencil closer to the paper. "I know it has a low chance of success, but I don't want to send you because you're on a countdown." His voice cracked on the last word. "I won't ask Ivy or Freddie to do what I must. They have enough on their minds."

Vic signed her name. "You're right." She didn't have the energy to argue. The last thing she wanted was to become another mog they would have to take down with their limited gicgauges.

He took the paper. "Wow, Sparks. Can I get that in writing too? I thought it would take a near-death experience before you'd admit I was right."

"Stuff it, muscles for brains." Vic shoved him, and he laughed. It was nice to hear.

"I'll see you later. Bomrosy somehow got some drinks, or she made them." He grimaced. "And the Nyx reapers are gathering in the workshop. We need a bit of time together before this begins. Will you come?"

"I don't think I have a choice since that's where I'm sleeping." Nothing like a bunch of drunk reapers to keep her awake all night.

His stance relaxed. "Good."

"I'll be in the workshop if you need me." She left with a wave and nodded at the reapers she passed.

Vic left the murmurs of the reapers behind and traipsed up the stairs to William and Samuel's room. She knocked on their door. When it opened, they were the only two in the room. They were working on building a cot since radiant didn't use magic. He might have to show her how it was done.

The room could sleep around five people, but there was no reason to stay in the bleak space, with basic stone walls and floor. The only fancy thing was the door. Since they had a communal bathroom, the rooms were for sleeping. It was no wonder other families wandered around the first floor. Being trapped in a room together for too long would be maddening.

"No one else here?" The only possessions here belonged to the brothers.

William smiled ruefully. "No one jumped at the chance to room with a radiant."

"I guess not everyone's as accepting as I am," Vic joked. Scraps approached her and rubbed against her leg. Vic picked him up, and he purred as she scratched his neck. "Thank you for hauling him down here. Poor guy's had to move around a lot."

"It might be a long time before we settle anywhere." William passed a board to his brother, who nailed it in place.

Vic hoped she would still be around to see the world settle, but unless they burned the entire city to the ground, it would take more time than she had left.

"On that note, why don't you come and get some drinks with me tonight? The reapers are gathering before we start our endless patrols. It's our last night."

He adjusted the frame, holding the corner joints together, and hesitated before responding, "Do you think I'd be wanted there?"

Vic hugged Scraps close to her. "Well, I want you there."

She stared into William's clear blue eyes. Her heart thudded. He had become special to her, and she wanted to spend her last days with him by her side. It might be selfish, but she couldn't let him go yet. After the party, she would tell him about the orb, but she wanted to feel normal for one night and forget about the noose around her neck.

"Then I'll be there." He brushed off his hands, and his lips curled into a grin.

"Good." Vic didn't know what to do, and she held a cat that wanted to be put down soon. "I'll see you tonight." She tried not to rush out of the room, but she turned before he could see her smile.

Back with Bomrosy, she ate a quick breakfast and spent the day organizing tools and trying her hand at building cots with the materials reapers had dropped off.

The fabric for the cot base slipped out of her hand, and she landed on her butt. She laughed when Bomrosy's arms wheeled out, and she fell too. Her friend joined in the laughter.

Bomrosy wheezed. "You'd think since I built a working light I could stretch out canvas for the base of a cot."

Xiona watched them with blank eyes, and they looked down at the cot that wouldn't hold anyone's weight. The canvas needed to be tightened on the base, but they'd built the frame too large.

"Okay, one more try, then I'm going to shower before the big party."

Bomrosy pulled the canvas tight. "We already made two. How are we getting worse?"

"No clue. Give me a mog any day. I guess we should have asked William for help."

At the mention of William, Bomrosy went silent.

Vic inserted the pins, and Bomrosy held the canvas taut. "You know he's sorry."

"I know."

Vic didn't push it. It was best that they worked it out themselves.

This time, they got the canvas pinned down.

Vic patted the cot. "I'll see tonight if I fall through. Is everyone from Nyx coming?"

There weren't many reapers from Nyx left, but it would be good to see them together and getting along.

"Yes. We haven't had much time to talk to them since they came together again at Haven," Bomrosy replied.

Bomrosy went over to a contraption on the shelf and poured the liquid into another glass container. The pungent alcohol smell crossed Vic's nose, and she coughed.

"Are you sure that isn't toilet cleaner?"

Bomrosy shut the lid, her eyes twinkling. "It might be good for that too."

"Blight have mercy." Vic took some clean clothes out of her pack and went to shower before everyone arrived. She would eat something first too and avoid drinking too much.

Her hair still drying, she helped Bomrosy set up slices of bread and fruit. The alcohol sat in clear containers stuffed with various fruits. Everyone would have to bring their own cup.

Nyx reapers filtered in. At first, it was awkward being around them—she'd never fit in with them, even before they'd stormed out of the Order—but as soon as some reapers pulled out instruments, the silence turned around, and they drank and laughed.

It wasn't hard to spot Ivy since her shadow, Freddie, stood behind her. He towered over everyone, and his shaved head reflected the light. Meeting him on the street, Vic would have thought that he could tear someone in two, but the gentle glow in his eyes as Ivy talked revealed more about his character. While he was stoic, Ivy was exuberant. She was short and curvy and likelier to rend someone in two. She spotted Vic across the crowded room and waved her over.

Ivy's glass was already full when Vic reached her.

"I'm glad you're here. I wanted to talk to you." Vic nodded her thanks as Freddie filled up her cup again.

Ivy's cheeks were rosy, and her freckles popped against the flush. "Not to talk me out of going?"

A weight settled in her heart, but she forced a smile and took a drink. "I know better than that. I wanted to thank you for helping at Haven and to apologize to you both for being a horrible team member. I should've trusted you. I'm sorry. Will you forgive me?"

Nodding, Freddie poured her another drink, and Ivy crashed into Vic with a hug, nearly spilling both their drinks. "I can understand why you didn't, and there isn't a need to ask. You're forgiven. Now let's drink tonight and enjoy each other!"

Still worried about their crazy mission, Vic cheered with the rest and sat across from them. The night went on, everyone drinking and laughing at stories about facing mogs and other reapers.

In the early hours, after everyone was more than drunk, they sat at the table, and Freddie took out a bag of stones.

Vic groaned at the drinking game. "I don't know if I'm up for this tonight."

"Hush now and just have fun." Ivy winked and waved at someone behind her. "William, Kai, join us for a game of dares!"

"Ivy!" Vic would have to apologize to her friend again for strangling her.

Freddie snorted but didn't help.

William and Kai came over and sat on either side of Vic, and she stared straight ahead. Bomrosy sat down too and chuckled at Vic.

"I've never played this before." William took a stone. They each had symbols and writing on them.

Ivy held up the stones. "It's pretty simple. You toss the stone on the table, and the stone nearest you is what you have to do. If it's a number, you take that many drinks. If it's a number and an arrow, you choose who takes the drink. If it's a scythe, you get an action dare from the group. If it's a wand, you have to tell the truth!"

"You don't have to play if you don't want to," Vic said, feeling hot between them.

William put his drink down. "It sounds like fun."

"Yeah! Let's go, reformed radiant!" Ivy handed him the cup with stones.

He shook it a few times, the stones rattling in the metal cup, then overturned it in the center of the table. The stones rolled out, and when they settled, everyone looked at the stone closest to them.

A stone with the number two and an arrow landed in front of Vic. She held it up and pointed to Ivy. "Two for you."

Ivy stuck out her tongue and held up a stone with a three and an arrow. "And three for you!"

They laughed and took their drinks. Freddie and Bomrosy drank on their own, and Kai groaned as he held up a scythe. Bomrosy whispered something to Ivy, and they both giggled. Vic was worried for a moment, but Bomrosy burst out, "Go give Landon a big ol' kiss."

Kai took a long drink. "Really, Bom, are you twelve?"

"Yep!" She continued to giggle against Ivy until they almost tipped over. Everyone at the table laughed, and Kai stood and glared at them. "Just you wait."

Bomrosy always teased Kai since Landon used to follow him around at the Order, but Kai approached the second with all his usual swagger, and before Landon knew what happened, Kai had kissed him on the cheek. The table cheered.

Landon raised his brows, shook his head at the group, and smacked Kai on the back. Everyone was tipsy enough that a few kisses between each other didn't matter.

As Kai came back, Bomrosy pouted. "That was such a copout."

He downed the rest of his drink. "Nothing more without permission."

The table clashed their glasses together. "To the gentleman!"

Ivy leaned over to William. "What did you get?"

He showed her the wand.

From the new snickers between Ivy and Bomrosy, Vic had a sinking feeling.

"Who in this room do you think should be with our dear Victoria?" Ivy asked and leaned in for the answer.

Vic couldn't help herself. She turned to look at him.

His face turned red as he met her eyes. "Me."

The room disappeared around her as she looked into his eyes. It might have been the drinks or the warmth from sitting next to him, but they leaned into each other. Her heart fluttered, and a shiver ran down her skin. William brushed his fingers down her bare arm, and heat trailed after his fingertips. The numbness from the drinks faded, and her entire body flared awake. The sound faded, and a light breath left her mouth as her eyes traced his lips. He drew closer to her. His other hand reached for her neck, but before their lips could meet, an arm crashed between them, spilling alcohol onto Vic and William. Kai gripped William's shirt and lifted him up.

"How are you better when you can't even protect her from herself?" Despite Kai's slurred words, she knew he was talking about her orb.

William tried to shove him away. "From herself? She can make up her own mind. She doesn't need you to do it for her."

"What's wrong with the two of you!" Vic pushed Kai back from William.

They tensed, ready to fight.

Vic stabbed her finger into Kai's chest. "You know I have enough to worry about, and you don't get to decide who I'm friends with."

Kai's jaw tightened. "You're just friends?"

Vic fanned her wet shirt from the spilled drink. "I'm just friends with you too."

Ivy snorted and took another shot. "Too many boyfriends? What a horrible problem. Just keep them both. It's the end of the world, after all."

Ivy hiccupped, and Freddie handed her water.

"Thanks for the advice." Vic turned to Kai and William. "Why don't you head out? It's late, and we're patrolling tomorrow."

Vic's mind blurred. She was tired and wanted to sleep off the end-of-the-world party.

"Fine, after him." Kai scowled at William.

"Blight, take us all," Vic muttered. She grabbed them by their shirts and shoved them out of the room together. The door banged shut behind them.

"That's right! You tell 'em who's in charge!" Ivy tipped over onto Freddie and promptly began to snore.

Bomrosy chuckled. "I wish I could fall asleep that fast."

"I think it's the alcohol."

Freddie picked up Ivy and nodded before leaving with her in his arms.

Bomrosy and Xiona were the only two left.

"I don't want them to go out into the swamp," Vic said.

"Same," Bomrosy agreed.

The two friends stood there, looking at the closed door, hoping for a bit of luck to follow Ivy and Freddie as they journeyed into the swamp.

4

WILLIAM

William stopped himself from clearing his throat as he sat across the table from Bomrosy. Her arms remained crossed over her chest, and her black eyes studied him. Xiona sat next to her, and Samuel stayed next to him. The offending ring lay on the table between them, shining in the workshop light and taunting them to uncover its secrets. He didn't know how this situation could get more uncomfortable, but he needed to work with Bomrosy to figure out if the radiant magic could be reversed.

"You radiant just use these without knowing what really happens?" Bomrosy glared at him and edged away from the ring like it might reach out and purify her too.

He reminded himself to remain calm. "I doubt I can relay all the years of study into a few minutes. But these were the answer to the curse of magic on Verrin. To keep us from the blight. To save us." He ended lamely. It sounded pathetic, even to him. Only a few weeks ago, he could have pompously told her about his beliefs, but they'd shattered with the information he'd found out about his father and the forced radiant army in Haven's belly. Now the whole radiant faith felt like a setup by GicCorp to turn people who worried about blight corruption into a compliant army.

Bomrosy picked up her toolbox from the floor and set it down with a loud thud, shaking the table. "I wish I knew where to begin." She opened the toolbox and took out pieces of shattered stones and one intact dull one without a spark of magic. "I've been spending my time with reapers, studying their stones. This one, which Vic brought me from the sewers, could be anything."

William picked up the gray stone. It didn't look magical. "This was found by the pile of ruins?"

"Maybe. I'll have to ask her again. It might be important, or it's likely just trash." She pulled more tools out of the box and laid them out one at a time with care. With a pair of tongs, she picked up his ring. "How does it feel when you use your magic?"

William pulled on the ends of his sleeves. "I can feel the blight being taken out of the person's body and released. Then it's like I put light inside them."

"Light?"

"It feels like a warm, sunny day?" William wasn't sure how to describe it to her.

"A feeling?" She glanced away from the ring and looked at the two radiant. "Can we assume they're happy, then?"

"They do smile." Although the blank eyes didn't say as much.

She placed the ring down. "That they do. So, we need a way to take out that light. Unless the rings take out more than blight?"

Radiant weren't called soul-suckers for nothing. "I

believe they're still in there. With my brother, the magic didn't stick. According to my father, he will try to harm me or others one day. That makes me think they're still there, just ... blocked."

"You're telling me your brother could go ballistic at any time?" Her hand inched toward a sharper tool.

"That's what my father claims, but he ended up saving me from getting purified." William didn't want to think that Samuel would harm anyone. "I'm keeping him with me. If something happens, it'll happen to me first."

"Good to know," Bomrosy muttered. She pushed the stones around. "If we can find out how the radiant stones are made, that might help us. Reapers take out blight, but they don't put anything back in the body. I wonder if this was supposed to replicate reaper gems but didn't quite get there."

The rings were man-made. There was no such thing as a first-generation ring. They all had the same amount of power and had to be emptied of blight before they could be used again.

"I don't suppose you know anyone at GicCorp willing to let us inside to see how the rings are made?"

William's mind wandered to Julian. "I do, but I'm not sure she's sympathetic to the reapers' cause."

Bomrosy chewed on her lip. "Maybe not to the reapers' cause, but maybe to a brother's?" She looked at Samuel pointedly.

"She might be, but she works in the sewers and funnels blight to Haven to get purified, and not many new rings are made per year. Do you think she'd have any connection to who makes them?"

Bomrosy tapped on the ring with a different tool. "Probably not." She dropped her tools and shoved away from the table, growling in frustration. "This is impossible. Tech makes more sense than this magic garbage."

William blinked. "Tech?"

"Yes. Even after all these years, I don't know how to make sense of a reaper's stone or fix it. I can't really test the working ones. If I mess up, it could kill the reaper."

"No, wait." William stood. "These are man-made. Wouldn't they be tech?"

Bomrosy plopped back into the chair and picked up the ring. "Yes, but the material isn't tech. Where do they get it? These are made with magic." Her eyes traveled to the broken reapers' stones. "These act like the stones from scythes."

"And like the wands," William added.

"What if they were both?"

The ring sat innocently on the table in front of them.

William's mind raced. "We just need to know how they make it."

Bomrosy rustled around in her toolbox and pulled out a bracelet. "What if we just needed to block the so-called light?"

"Block the light?"

"I made these to counter a signal sent between a ring and a bracelet. What if I could block what's keeping them locked up inside?"

William didn't understand anything about tech, but he was willing to be Bomrosy's sounding board. "With the ring and bracelet, you knew what it connected to and attached it together. How can your device block something inside them?"

Bomrosy muttered to herself, gathered the stones, and went to her workbench. She turned on a lamp and bent over the ring. William stayed next to Samuel, who sat smiling, just like Xiona.

"When she gets like this, nothing can break her concentration."

William started at Vic's voice. He hadn't heard the door open. Her hair was damp from the shower, and her eyes had dark smudges underneath them. She looked wonderful. He swallowed. "I don't think I was much help."

Vic put her dirty clothes in a bag next to her cot on the floor. "If anyone can help her understand the radiant magic, it's you." She sat on the cot and leaned against the stone wall.

William left Samuel's side and sat on the floor next to her. "I don't want to get my hopes up that she can reverse it. But then we would have to figure out how to stop magic from infecting them."

"One problem at a time, Sally Sunshine."

The old insult made his heart leap. "How are you doing?"

Vic smiled weakly. "Hungover. But I suppose we need to talk."

William gestured at Bomrosy. "Should we go somewhere else?"

Vic nodded, then winced as William stood. He put his hand out for her to grab. He had a feeling she was about to let him down easy. After he'd told the truth last night, he thought there'd been a moment between them. What if he'd imagined it?

He pulled on his sleeves. He would've been happy to support her as a friend, but Kai had made it an issue last night, and there was no taking his words back. He knew she liked Kai, probably as more than a friend. Eventually, she would forgive Kai since they made more sense together. William wasn't a fighter like them.

They left and walked down the tunnels. Samuel shadowed them from a distance. They found an alcove and leaned against the wall, waiting for the other to talk.

Vic pulled her hair over her shoulder. "It's almost refreshing talking about relationships when we're in the middle of a civil war." Sad humor lit her face.

"We are engaged, aren't we?" William said lightly.

It had the desired effect, and she laughed. "How could I forget?" Too soon, the sadness was back. "I didn't want to tell anyone, and now I'm telling everyone." She ran her finger along the scar on her neck. "I don't have an orb, William."

His chest tightened.

"This may be a cheap way to do things, but I don't want to lead you on." She swallowed heavily. "I can only offer you friendship since I don't know how much time I have left. Anything romantic would just hurt you."

Where had all the air gone? William felt adrift. He wished this was a nightmare, but under her scar, if he looked close enough, there was no telltale lump under the skin.

"That's why I'm teamed up with Kai. When I can no longer be drained of blight, he will ... make things easier for me."

"Kill you?" Panic assailed him, and his hand shook.

"Damn, light stick, you don't pull any punches."

"We could purify you and figure out what to do about the orb after we help the others. As always, you're being way too brash. I know you're strong enough, but let me help you."

"I can't do it. I'm sorry."

"That's selfish." William wanted to stop his angry words, but he couldn't. "You say you trust Bomrosy to come up with a solution, then trust her. Death? You would rather die than become a radiant? Don't you think that's extreme? Just because you've always hated the radiant doesn't mean you should die to avoid it. We can fix this." The words spilled out frantically as he tried to convince her. She couldn't be serious.

Tears formed in her eyes. "I'm afraid. I—"

He pulled her into his arms. "Don't choose this. Trust me. Trust Bomrosy."

She shook but didn't respond. William wanted to press her to talk to him and get her to agree, but that would only make her dig her heels in deeper. He rested his cheek against the top of her head. It would be okay. She was still here and alive. They could fix this together.

After a while, she nudged him, and he let her go.

"I never get to be the tough reaper in front of you." Her eyes were red, and it broke him that he couldn't do anything to help.

He ran his hands up and down her arms. "If anything, I want you to feel like I can be an escape from all this." The words felt weak to him, but her face brightened.

"Thanks."

They walked back to the workshop in silence. She waved at him as she disappeared behind the door. They'd solved nothing, and it left an emptiness in him. She never saw his side about being a radiant.

"I might have to work with the enemy, Samuel."

Samuel smiled and followed William to Kai's room.

WILLIAM KNOCKED ON THE DOOR, AND A FROWNING KAI answered.

"I'm needed in a meeting. What do you want?"

William matched his frown. "I see you didn't become commander based on your social skills."

Kai remained in the doorway. "I'll let you know when they have the next personality audition for reapers." He grabbed the door to shut it.

William held up his hand. "I need to talk to you about Vic."

Kai paused. "Does she know you're here?"

"Can I come in?"

For a moment, William thought Kai wouldn't let him in, but Kai held the door open. His room was bare and smaller than William's, but it was large enough for one. Only a few items sat on the shelf, and everything was neat. William appreciated being organized, but it was easier since everyone had left most of their belongings behind.

"Done with your inspection? I do need to leave soon, so what do you want to talk about?" The man actually tapped his foot at him.

William didn't want to be here either, so he got to the point. "Are you really going to kill Vic if she transforms?"

Only a flicker in Kai's eyes told William his question shocked the commander.

"She told you?"

"Bomrosy and I are working on radiant magic. Can't you convince her it would be the better option?"

Kai's face stilled. "I can't say that would be the better option. What if you never figure out how to reverse it?"

William clenched his hands into fists. "Even if we can't reverse it within a month, we might within a year or two. Blight, maybe three. She'll spend three years as a radiant. What's so terrible about that?"

"Are you suggesting we force it on her? Got a taste for it, radiant?"

"What are you implying?" William's blood simmered. How dare he assume his intentions. He already felt guilty enough. He didn't need this man's judgment.

Kai smirked. "Just suggesting that someone might take after their dad."

William forced the anger down and took a deep breath. "I won't force her. I just think she needs to hear it from someone else. If you're ready to kill her, so be it. I'm not giving up on her." William stomped to the door, but Kai caught his arm.

"I'm not giving up on her either."

William yanked his arm away. "Sure." He left Kai's room and stormed around the apartments. People avoided him and his brother as he walked off his anger. He still had time to convince Vic. If they found a way to reverse Sam's condition and return him to his old self, they could help all the radiant. But first, they needed to mimic the gicorbs. One problem at a time. He wouldn't give up on his fire girl.

"I won't let her die."

"Do what you must."

V ic held the giant net and quirked her eyebrows at Kai. "We're going to throw these on radiant, then what?"

"First, we have them follow us past the river. I don't think we can drag them over the ledge without them pulling us in. Then we bring them back here and lock them up until Bomrosy finds a way around the purification."

"How're we going to feed all these new mouths?"

Kai put a net in his pack and zipped it shut. "You might be too optimistic about how many we'll catch. Most reapers are on mog duty and charge support."

For now, they were escorting people above ground to charge. The allied founders in the city were investigating GicCorp to see if the corporation was monitoring credit use at the charging stations. They were using founder credits to charge, but if GicCorp was watching, it would notice the increase in charging.

"They aren't fighters."

"Sometimes, that's worse."

"True." Radiant would keep fighting, even if they were severely injured. Vic finished packing her own net and adjusted her scythe on her back. It wasn't the most comfortable, but she could put up with it for a few hours.

Kai pulled on his bag. "Are you sure you should take your scythe? If you can't limit how much the stone holds, it might break or drain you again."

"I can still use it to fight with." She wanted to add that it didn't matter if she drained herself, but it was best not to broach the subject of her gicorb.

He looked like he wanted to say something, then stopped. "Up to you."

"Go ahead, fearless leader." Vic hooked her thumbs under the pack's straps. They'd brought extra supplies in case they couldn't head back to base. All the reapers had been warned to make sure no one followed them.

They left the base, nodding at Janesa when she opened the glass door. They looped around different paths before making their way to the sewers near Haven. The commanders wanted them to always approach from different directions so GicCorp couldn't pinpoint the base's location. The potent smell of sewage clung to them, but the skittering sounds of rats told them they were the only humans in these tunnels. When it felt safe, they veered to where the tunnel's rock smoothed out and the lights glowed brighter. There weren't many places to hide in the tunnels near Haven, and Vic didn't want to jump into the sewage river again.

Keeping his voice quiet, Kai asked, "Sparks?"

"Yeah?"

"These last days have been hectic. We haven't had time to talk about your orb."

Vic bit her tongue to keep from groaning. "Do we have to talk about it again?"

"I'd rather come to a solution that would make us both happy."

"It's not your body, Kai."

He sighed. "I know. I'm not telling you what to do, but I'm asking you not to be so extreme. Why are you so afraid of radiant?"

"Their souls are gone. If my soul's gone, I want my body gone too." She shouldn't have asked Kai to kill her if she started to turn into a mog. Maybe when the veins darkened in her eyes, she should go over the wall.

Kai walked on, not looking at her. "We don't know if their souls are gone. That's just a rumor. William believes his brother's still in there."

"Sam's different, and his behavior doesn't match the rest of the radiant."

He branched off to the left and paused before walking farther into the tunnel. "You already think Bomrosy will fail?"

Why did this always turn to her trust in her friends? She believed in Bomrosy, but in reversing radiant, there probably wasn't a solution. "I don't want to talk about this. When I get worse, how about you and everyone else who has an opinion sit down and we can talk? Right now, I'm trying to keep my family safe from the Nordics. I can't think about orbs." Her voice trembled, and she hated how it gave her emotions away. "I'm trying to be strong here. Let me."

"Okay. I'll drop it."

Vic's chest tightened. "I panicked when I asked you. William's right. I should trust Bomrosy. I want to believe their souls are still in there."

Kai jumped over a line of water, scaring a rat into the darkness. He glanced back at her, looking like he was debating with himself. "So, you and the reformed radiant?"

"Can we talk about anything else?" Why was he bringing up William? It wasn't like she had a future left.

"Blight, Sparks. What am I allowed to talk about?"

"Verrin's impending doom?"

Kai chuckled. "That's old news. I want to hear about you and the night light."

"I doubt that." Things were still tense between her and Kai. She couldn't deny he was attractive. The way he moved like a predator, the way he fought, and his banter—there was so much to like about him. But by the easy way he'd pushed her aside, she got the feeling he didn't think she was equal to him, and that nagged at her.

They stopped at the river and inched carefully along the side.

"Why not? Aren't we buddies?"

"I don't know what we are." Vic wanted his friendship, but maybe it was impossible.

"Almost lovers?"

"Eh, I never liked your butt that much."

"The night light has a good butt?"

"He might. I've never seen it."

"Early stages?"

Vic pointed ahead. "Look, there's the junk pile."

They jumped down from the ledge onto the shore, and Kai stopped in front of her. He gently tugged on her hair. "You deserve to be happy, Sparks. I'm a bit mad at myself for messing things up between us."

His warm eyes melted her. He was Kai, and it was fire and sparks, but in the chaos of the city, William was her anchor. In a different world, would she have waited for Kai? She still felt that gentle tug when he looked at her, but that was different from the warmth she felt with William.

"Sometimes, when things burn too hot, they go out quickly." The words left her mouth, and something settled insider her.

"Ouch."

They stood there, looking at each other as if trying to figure out what they were. As she stared into his eyes, she saw his regret at pushing her aside, but there was nothing deeper than that. There was physical attraction, but that wasn't enough to keep them afloat. Kai brushed his fingers along her face, and his guarded expression melted away. He leaned in and brushed his lips against her forehead.

In a whisper she could barely hear, he said, "He better deserve you."

Vic arched her neck back and softly kissed his cheek. "He does."

In the quietness, she watched his battle of emotions as he put up his guard again to hide his sadness. She blinked back her tears and looked away.

Keeping her voice light, she said, "Fine, will you feel better if I say you have a nice butt?"

"Wouldn't hurt." The mood returned slowly back to normal.

"Kai, from the moment I first saw you slinking across the canal, I thought to myself, 'Blight, I could bounce pebbles off that butt.' Better?"

"Slinking?"

"You were trying to arrest an innocent freelancer. So yes, you were all slinky." Vic mimed his walk, but she came across more like a mog without proper legs, and he laughed.

Kai blinked. "Oh good, that's exactly what I was going for. You missed out, but after the first year of reaper training, we do slink training. Nyx reapers also need to have general appeal among the masses. Our goal is to be the slinkiest."

Vic snorted, and the pressure in her chest lessened. She poked him. "I guess that's why all the hotties pick Nyx."

"It's good to see you smile again."

"You too." It might not be easy, but Vic knew they would be okay.

Kai smiled and turned back. They continued to walk. The large dome, filled with twisted metal and dull gems, had become a landmark for the reapers in the sewers. The old path into Haven was blocked now, but the other tunnels remained. William said the Nordics had used the tunnels when they'd kept him captive for a short time. The other patrols kept track of which tunnels they explored. Vic and Kai got the first one to the left of the sewage river. They might not find anyone in these tunnels, but they were still under GicCorp and next to Haven. If anything, they could report any activity they saw. If they broke into Haven again, Vic could help Maddox, the daughter of the Stone founder, who'd gotten sent to Haven for helping Vic. She hoped Maddox hadn't been part of the fight with the founders, telling herself that Tristan wouldn't use a radiant the founders would recognize.

They didn't talk anymore to avoid making a sound in the smooth tunnels. The air felt tense as they walked down the path, and any scuff of their boots sounded too loud. They planned to take the first branch off and mark the tunnels they explored in the next few nights. About thirty minutes had passed when they hit their first side tunnel.

"That took a while," Kai whispered.

Vic pulled out a bottle of paint from her pack and made a tiny dot in the upper right corner of the entrance. The right corner signified which side to turn to get back to the main tunnel, since on their way back it would be on their left. She put the paint container in her pocket and followed Kai. The tunnel looked like the others; as long as they marked them, they shouldn't get lost.

The quiet continued until voices cut in and out ahead of them. Kai signaled for them to pick up their pace. They ran as silently as possible toward the sound. The talking increased in volume, and the path came to a door ajar. She and Kai crouched and peered into the room. Vic held back a gasp. Two men were arguing. One of them was Tristan, and the other her father.

Her wide eyes met Kai's, his surprise mirroring her own. She was just starting to trust her father. Why would he be meeting with Tristan down here? If he was keeping up appearances, they should have met out in Verrin, not in dark sewer tunnels.

The voices were too muddled for Vic to make out the words, and from the look of concentration on Kai's face, she figured he wasn't having much luck either.

"Hear something interesting?"

They slowly turned their faces up to see a man standing over them. With no time to think, Kai kicked the person's knees, buckling them. Then they ran.

Shouts echoed behind them as they navigated the tunnel back to the river. Vic didn't dare look back to see if anyone had joined the man. Tristan probably wouldn't chase them. He had other people to do it for him. Would this put her mother and sister in danger? Fear molded around her as she pumped her legs. Kai skidded to a stop at the river and pulled her up onto the ledge. She was glad he'd paid attention to their location. Thoughts of her sister had stolen her concentration.

They made it back to the main tunnel, and the sounds of pursuit hadn't followed them.

"Did they stop?" No sooner had Vic asked than a low moan came from the river. They hadn't considered Tristan's mog army.

"Blight. Go ahead of me." Kai ran behind Vic.

Since his scythe still had a gauge, he could wear the mog down before Vic helped—if they couldn't outrun it.

Squelching sounds rose from behind them, and Vic figured this was a more agile mog. They needed to find a good place to make their stand away from the base.

A narrow doorway appeared ahead of them.

"Here?" she asked.

"Okay!"

Slowing, Vic pulled out her scythe and flicked it open. An answering flick came from behind her. They turned, and Kai threw off his pack to free his movements, and Vic followed suit.

The mog loped on long black limbs. The corrupted skin broke open with the monster's movements. It was smaller for a mog, but Vic knew why Tristan had chosen it. Its speed was abnormal. If Tristan could make fast mogs, they'd have another problem to add to their list.

Wasting no time, Kai slashed at the creature's front legs. His scythe gleamed with the cut, but the mog pushed back on its haunches, leaped over his second attempt, and plowed into Vic. Heat flared from her scythe as the blade met the mog's flesh. Ignoring its growing wound, the mog pushed its full weight onto Vic's scythe, gnashing its teeth inches from her face. The mog's claws sank into her stomach, and Vic screamed.

Her arms strained, and its breath smelled like rotten meat as dark drool dripped from its mouth onto her. Kai hooked the bottom of his blade around its neck and pulled, draining the mog and slicing off its head. It fell to the side, its teeth barely moving as the last of the blight drained away, leaving Vic under a pile of bones and slime.

Kai flicked his scythe shut and ran to her. Vic flinched in pain as he checked for injuries. He reached for his bag and pulled out bandages.

"Stay with me, Sparks."

Vic saw a red haze as Kai pulled apart her shirt and staunched the flow of blood from her abdomen.

"How bad?" she gasped as he wrapped her wounds.

Kai didn't respond, working quickly as Vic took shallow breaths. He put their scythes and bags onto his back, then picked Vic up. She almost passed out. Her skin burned with pain, and she was afraid her stomach looked like it had gone through a meat grinder. She dared to look down. The bandages were soaked through with blood.

Kai held her as he ran. Vic could tell he was trying to be gentle, but she felt every jarring movement when his feet hit the ground. Vic almost wished she would pass out, but the pain digging into her kept her awake. It felt like hours had passed when they ran by the imb guarding the door to the room with healers.

It was a small staff, made up of a few imbs who had reapers in their family. Two women took her from Kai and gave her something for the pain. A comforting numbness entered her body, and one woman brushed Vic's sweaty hair from her forehead.

"Rest."

Finally, a painless nothingness entered her mind, and she blacked out.

Someone was stroking Vic's hair as she blinked her eyes open. She turned her face and heard Scraps's rumbling purrs as he licked her hair.

Vic groaned as she tried to move, but a hand stopped her.

"Take it easy and let me help you. You don't want to use your middle to push up." William gently helped her sit up against the wall. The cot was narrow and functional, and a few more lined the room, with basically no privacy. Samuel sat to the side, looking at nothing.

"Kai needed to meet with the commanders, so he asked me to sit with you."

"You didn't need to do that." Vic tried to get a full breath, but the bandages restricted her. "How'd you get Scraps down here?"

"Since you're the first injured person they've had to deal with, they let him in this one time." The cat purred as William scratched his ears.

Vic smiled. "He has full control of you."

William chuckled. "What are we but servants to cats?"

"True." Vic pulled up the blanket. "When can I leave?"

"The healer said I could help you to your room as soon as you woke up. Just no patrol tonight and"—he indicated a pack next to the bed—"you'll need to change your bandages."

"A lot of help I am already off patrol." She took the pack of fresh bandages and lifted the bottom of her shirt. "I don't think I can do this by myself. Can you help me?"

"Ah, sure." His face reddened as he lightly picked at the old bandages.

Vic bit her lip. "It'll go faster if you just cut them off."

"Ah, yes, yes, you're right."

She didn't laugh when his face turned even redder as he cut away the bandages, but when his fingers brushed her exposed skin, it was her turn to heat up. She turned her face away, and he sucked in a breath at the sight of the wounds.

"This is bad."

"Thanks. I figured that one out."

His blue eyes narrowed. "You are being careful, aren't you? You aren't—"

"Trying to die on purpose? No, Will, I'm not. There are easier ways to go than letting a mog maul me." She tried to keep her voice light, but he frowned.

"It's not a joke, Vic." He gently wrapped her middle in new bandages. The healing soaked into her skin, and she sighed.

"I'm sorry. That wasn't kind of me."

He pressed his lips to the top of her head, and her skin tingled.

"I'm not letting you go that easily," he whispered.

She reached for William's hand, but he instead put his

arm around her back and pulled her so she was nearly pressed against him as she stood. His clean linen scent still drifted around him, even though they were down in the tunnels. Her face felt hot, and she stepped away, but his arm halted her. She kept telling herself not to let anything happen, but after her talk with Kai, things with William felt more real and harder to say no to. Could she be that selfish and be with him, even though she was about to die?

William kept his arm around her back but shifted to her side. "Samuel, can you grab Scraps and the pack?"

Without responding, his brother picked up the items and followed them out of the healers' room. He acted as if nothing had happened.

"William?"

"Yes?"

Vic glanced around the empty halls as they walked toward the stairs. "I need to see my father."

"Now?" he answered in hushed tones.

"As soon as I can walk."

Now it was William's turn to look around the empty base. "I don't think the commanders will let you."

"There's a sewer line right next to the Glass house. It's a risk, but I have to confront my father. If he's not really helping us, we could all be in danger."

His fingers twitched against her arm. "Wouldn't that put you in danger too?"

"He's keeping something from me." Vic didn't think he'd betrayed them. But why had he met with Tristan? It was time for her father to tell her. If something happened to him, she needed to know what was going on so she could protect her mother and sister.

"Fine, but I'm going with you."

Vic tilted her head at Samuel. "Where will your brother go?"

"He'll have to stay behind."

"If he'll listen."

They arrived at the workshop, and a tired Bomrosy got up from her workbench to greet them. "Heard you got a vicious mog?"

Vic sighed with relief as she sat at the table.

Without a word, William left the room with Samuel.

Vic frowned but replied to Bomrosy, "It was a fast one."

Bomrosy's brow furrowed as she sat across from Vic. "That's strange."

"I don't want to know if GicCorp found a way to make super mogs."

Her friend zoned out, which meant she was thinking about how it would be possible. Bomrosy shook her head. "There isn't a way to control how a mog forms—that we know of. But who knows what GicCorp's hiding behind its walls?"

William came back with food and set it in front of Vic. "You'll need it."

Bomrosy looked between them, missing nothing. "Okay, what are you both planning?"

Vic almost choked on her food. "You know me too well." She swallowed. "I'm going to see my father tonight, and William's helping."

Bomrosy rolled her eyes. "I suppose that means I'm on Samuel duty?"

"If you don't mind."

She pushed herself away from the table. "So much for keeping him with you."

Vic gave William a questioning look, but he shook his head. "I shouldn't be long. Right, Vic?"

Bomrosy waved them off. "I won't waste my time telling you it's dangerous to go above ground and that this is foolish. I'm just going to work on my project, knowing that someone's too stubborn to listen to me anyway."

"Thanks, Bomrosy."

She bent over her workbench and handled her tools with a bit more force than usual.

"Go ahead and finish, then get some rest. I'll come by later to get you."

"Okay."

William left with Samuel, and Vic's eyelids grew heavy as she finished her meal. She soon passed out on her cot, and when she woke again, her stomach only hurt a bit.

She rubbed her eyes. Bomrosy hadn't moved from the bench. "What time is it?"

Bomrosy paused at the sound of Vic's voice. "It's hard to tell down here, isn't it?" She shuffled through her tools and found a clock. "Almost night. I left some supper for you on the table. Do you need help up?"

"No, but I do need help changing these." Vic stood and handed her pack to Bomrosy. She hadn't changed out of her old shirt, and it was so torn that the bandages did a better job of covering her. She took it off.

Bomrosy cut the old bandages away and whistled. "What a mess it left."

"Thanks," Vic replied dryly.

Bomrosy wrapped her wounds, and the freshly imbued bandages tingled, making Vic feel more normal.

As Vic hunted for another shirt, the door squeaked open,

and William walked in. He turned red when he saw Vic only in bandages, and she hurriedly pulled the shirt on.

"Sorry." William closed his eyes, then almost ran into the table.

Bomrosy snorted. "Knock next time."

He cleared his throat. "Are you ready?"

Vic gently put on her harness, careful of where she placed the straps. "Yes."

"Samuel, stay here with Bomrosy and Xiona." Samuel didn't answer him, but he stayed in the room.

William walked next to her. "Do you think they'll let us out?"

"We aren't prisoners." Vic waved to the imb on duty when they left the base. "They trust us to know how much danger we're in."

"Yet here we go back into Verrin."

Vic pointed at the glass door. "Want to go back?"

William huffed. "No."

Vic laughed at his contrite face. "We'll be careful. If something happens, we'll run and meet up at Kai's old place."

"Neither of us is in the best shape to run."

"Then we'll just have to not get caught."

"Perfect."

William pulled at his sleeves, and Vic smiled. He was the same, but so different from when she'd first met him. He looked better and more approachable in clothes that weren't white. He'd changed the day he'd purified his brother. It was a change for the better, but the cost was high.

"What happened between you and your father?"

William rubbed the back of his neck. "I took away his

ring and told him to leave Samuel and me alone. I also might have cut off his finger ..."

Vic almost ran into a support pole. "You cut off his finger?"

"I used my wand to shrink the metal, and well, yeah, it cut all the way through."

"And I thought my family relationships were bad."

"It's amazing we turned out so normal," William deadpanned.

"Truly."

He veered out of the way of a cobweb. "It doesn't matter that I wrecked his ring. I'm sure they'll give him another, and he'll keep doing what he's doing."

"I'm sorry." She could relate a bit, since she was worried that her father might be working with Tristan.

"There's nothing to be sorry about."

"I know, but it was your whole life. Then the lies and your brother. Even though I didn't really care for you when we met, I wouldn't wish this on anyone."

He put his hands in his pockets. "We're all living in the founders' game. They're the only ones who know what's happening, and we're living and dying while they run the show."

Vic hooked her arm in his, and his eyes widened in surprise. "It does feel that way. Maybe our rebellion won't amount to anything, but at least we won't go quietly."

"I hope that makes enough of a difference." He bumped his head against hers. "To think I was ready to meet my future wife and tame her to be a good radiant woman."

"Gross."

"Agreed." He sighed. "I don't know how I could stand being around myself. I was an ass."

"The first step to fixing a mistake is admitting it."

The ladder to the entrance was ahead of them.

"This is it," Vic said. "I might need you to do the heavy pushing."

William climbed and peered out of the grate. Since it was nearly dark, no one would be out, especially now that there were no reapers. The city didn't know that Tristan could control mogs, but it wasn't worth it to break the curfew.

"All clear."

He quietly pushed the grate off and climbed out, then helped Vic out and replaced the grate. The grate they'd chosen was a bit farther than the one next to the Glass house. Vic worried someone might be watching it. They hustled into an alley and followed it toward the Glass house. They glanced around for any threats. Now, in the quiet streets, every sound seemed to announce their presence.

The silence broke when Vic heard the steady marching of feet on the main road before the alley ended. These wouldn't be citizens. Vic pulled William to the side, and they hunkered down next to a pile of broken wooden boxes. Through the gaps in the trash, Vic saw the main road. The marching got louder, and her heart pounded to the ominous beat. William pressed against her back to make them blend into the pile of trash. His breath tickled the back of her neck.

People dressed in red marched in a row of six, with one person behind them. They all had a black cloth sash, except for the person in the back, who wore a hood large enough to cover their face. Vic couldn't see clearly, but she would bet money the six people were radiant. The hooded figure's head turned left to right. The loose clothing hid their body shape. Their pants were tucked into tall black boots, and they had a wand holster across their chest. A shiver went from her neck through her body when the person glanced down the alley. They weren't a radiant. The shadowed face turned away, and Vic took a shaky breath. The sounds of the group faded, but Vic remained crouched with William.

"Who was in the back?" William whispered.

"Someone we don't want to run into."

William backed away, leaving her back cold, even in the evening heat. Her stomach twinged as she stood. She crossed her arms. William's face showed concern.

"We should move before another patrol comes through." Vic kept her voice low, but it still sounded too loud.

Walking silently, they skirted the street to the next alley that connected to the Glass house. At least with the marching radiant, they could hear them coming.

The Glass house radiated light from inside, sticking out in the dimly lit Verrin. Vic and William ran to the gate and squeezed through.

Vic led him to the side door in case another founder was in her home. The door led to the kitchen, and it smelled like remnants of dinner and soap. The help would be gone by now, but Vic looked around before going into the next room.

In the hall, the light was on in her father's office. She quietly knocked and heard a "come in" from inside.

Now that she was here, Vic didn't know what to do. The urge to find out why her father had met with Tristan had driven her here, but the fragile growth of her and his relationship gave her pause. With cold fingers, she opened the door.

Her father's dark red hair was mussed, and his jacket lay haphazardly on the desk. He fiddled with the colored sand on his desk. From the square sandbox on his desk, he made sharp glass spikes grow and bend.

His green eyes flicked to Vic, but a weighty sadness met her and not surprise. Had he expected her to come tonight?

Red splotches stained the left arm of his white sleeve.

Vic rushed into the room. "Are you hurt?"

Her father looked between her and William. "You both better sit down. There are things I need to tell you. Things I thought I could protect you from, but I'm running out of time."

"What do you mean, out of time?" Vic pointed to his arm. "Don't you need to treat that? What happened? Why were you with Tristan last night?"

Her father held up his hand. "I'll tell you as much as I can, but certain elements are magically hard for me to tell." He tapped a thin line of glass he was growing, and it shattered to the desk.

"I don't understand."

"I will explain that too, if I can."

"Why now?"

Her father broke off more glass with his wand with angry stabs. "The radiant situation is out of hand. I'm powerless to stop it since I can't run at full capacity with my magic. I planned to go down to the base tomorrow and tell you these things since it isn't safe for you here, but you found me first in the tunnels." He smiled. "You are my daughter."

"You knew I was there?"

He tapped his wand on the desk. "The guard didn't have

to go into much detail before we figured it out. Now I'm going to tell you something you might not believe. Our history has been controlled and hidden, and everything is based on lies."

"That makes it simple," William muttered.

Her father's lips twitched. "It does sound dramatic."

Vic's mind spun. "How do you know your version of history is correct?"

"Because I was there at the beginning."

Vic's fingers bit into her palms. "At the beginning? Of what?"

"Of Verrin."

Vic glanced at William, his face pale. "Just how old are you?"

"Old."

"Your body has held up. Are we talking hundreds of years?"

"Thousands." He touched his bloody sleeve. "And this isn't my original body. It's one of many I've had over the years."

Vic swallowed as her brain struggled to understand how it was possible. "Is this just you? Whose body is it?"

"We're a select group inside of GicCorp. Our bodies come from the vitals who are sent to Haven. The bodies are turned into radiant to weaken the soul but keep the body alive." He struggled to get the words out. "We are all reapers, but we need non-reaper bodies with souls to come back in. We call ourselves the originators."

"What?" Vic almost shouted.

Her father held up his hand again. "Their souls are shut away after the first year, then our souls are placed inside them. With the way the powers work, the bodies last longer, and when the body's original family dies, we blend into the Nordic family line with some reason or another, like a passed-down relic or through a shocking marriage to a commoner."

Vic found it hard to listen. "No one in Haven is purifying magic? The vitals are there so you can steal their bodies? What happens to the blight?" She could hear her own tremble of rage in her questions.

"The blight?" Her father pointed to the sky. "It stays over the city. We've never cared much about blight since it can't infect reapers."

She touched her neck, and William clasped her other hand. "I won't get infected?"

Her father reached for her, but she pulled back. "No, your charge only dampened your powers to drain blight. I should've told you, but things needed to play out a certain way."

"I thought I was going to die." Relief and shock scrambled her mind. William's hand anchored her to the world. But if this wasn't her father's body ... did he have another family long ago? How many families did he have?

"Who are you? Who's my real father?" Her voice grew into a shriek, and she realized she was standing over her father with her hands braced on his desk.

Without breaking eye contact, he rolled up the cuffs of his shirt to his elbow. Under it was a thick bandage. He unwrapped it, inch by inch. Black glass was embedded in the flesh of his arm. Without the bandage, blood spattered on the desk.

Vic stared at his arm. "I don't know what this means."

Her father pressed into the glass, causing more blood to

coat it. She reached to stop him, but William held her back. He continued to press, and pain ran over his face.

"Stop it!"

Her father gasped. "I have to. This body was defective, and the soul still clings to it. If we take their soul out completely, we can't put our souls inside. It's almost like we have to earn our right to take the body. Normally, the soul's very weak, then it fades. But when I mention it, or think of it, or even talk to it, it fights me. Pain's the only way to make it retreat and keep me here. I don't know ... how long ... I can answer ... you." He raised his hand to touch her jaw. "I've done every-thing evil ... everything ... but it was you ... my family ... I was supposed to get a new ... body ... but I fell ... in love ... and Tristan didn't ... like that." He dropped his hand and squeezed his arm tighter, and the glass punched into his palm. "You made me want ... to be better..." A tear ran down his face. "You may be his in body ... but you're mine ... in soul."

The door crashed open. Vic jumped and reached for her scythe on her back, but her mother came into the room with a light blue glass bottle. Without a word, she rushed to her husband, opened his mouth, and tipped the liquid in. Her mother gently held his head and placed it on the desk as he passed out.

"Your father has been fighting the soul since he entered the body. I wish I had more to tell you, but like he said, if he talks about it too much, it fights him. Sometimes pain isn't enough to stop it." Her mother brushed his hair softly. "His refusal to take another body put him in a dangerous posi-tion. Tristan saw it as a betrayal that he'd choose a tempo-rary family over him. Their friendship goes back to the beginning. And Tristan can hurt him through us. Your father tried to act cold toward you and Emilia." Her mother sighed. "That part might have worked a little too well. He wanted this to be his last body and die surrounded by the family he loves."

"You knew too?"

Her mother pulled out a fresh bandage from the drawer and wrapped her father's arm. "Yes, Victoria." She slouched over her husband. "I know about his fight with the originators of Verrin." When she was done wrapping his arm, she pulled a blanket out from the desk drawer and covered him, then went around the desk to face Vic and William. "He thought he could protect us against them on his own. I supported him, even though he was being foolish. How could he tell people about what is happening in Haven? That they turn people into radiant and steal their bodies after a year, before their souls fade too much? Who would believe it?"

"I still don't believe it."

Her mother tugged on Vic's arm. "I wish I could say more, but you've been here too long. Tristan's monitoring us, and it might already be too late."

Vic put her scythe back in her harness, not realizing it had fallen to the ground, and they went to the side door. She paused. "Father's a reaper? Like me?"

Her mother's face softened, and she touched the folded scythe in Vic's hand. "Whose scythe do you think you inherited?"

Too many feelings crashed inside her. Swallowing thickly, she nodded to her mother, and they ran out the door. Vic turned to see her mother framed in the light of the house. The house she hated. The house with its rules and expectations. Now they all seemed so silly. It was all a front? The way her father had been harsh with her and his disappointment when she'd become a reaper? What was real? Was it wrong to care for a man who was killing another soul inside him? What did that say about her morals?

Her hand brushed against the glass walls as she left through the gate and ducked into the alley.

"Do you need a moment?" William asked.

"I need a century, but I don't think I'm on the list to have that much time."

William stayed close beside her as they snuck through the alley. "Now I'm certain about the blighted radiant calling."

Vic put a hand on his arm as they approached the end of the alley. "But you also know the soul is still there. Sam is still inside."

He blinked his blue eyes, and hope filled them. "You're right. Sam's there." Worry showed on his face. "Your father never mentioned if purification can be reversed."

"You and Bomrosy can find a way."

"Does that mean you'll trust us?"

"I wanted to believe that the soul was still inside, but the way they look scares me. And the thought of not being in control ..." A chill traveled across her skin. "We'll figure out how to get them back." They had at least a year. That was longer than most. Those who had been radiant for longer than a year might not be so lucky.

Vic listened for the sound of marching, but the main street was empty. They rushed to get to the final grate that led back into the sewers. The irony of wanting to be under the city with the smell of waste wasn't lost on Vic. Somehow, that smelly base had become her real haven.

They made it to the next alley, but two large mogs, with a hooded figure standing between them, blocked it.

Vic couldn't make out the face, but she recognized the deep voice. "I knew you would come back this way."

Tristan pulled off his hood, revealing his usual slicked-down hair that remained perfect despite the hood. In the dark alley, his eyes looked more ancient, and the puzzle in Vic's mind fell into place. She was fighting a man who had lived for thousands of years. Years to perfect magic as an imb and reaper. How could she even compete? William pulled out his wand, and she flicked open her scythe. Nothing like two ants approaching a giant.

The mogs blinked slowly next to him. They were bulkier, with long limbs that would give them speed. The mogs' mouths hung open, showing off their sharp, yellowing teeth.

"Nice night for a walk, isn't it, Tristan?"

He flashed his white teeth at her, and the smile contained a predatory air. "I didn't think you'd be foolish enough to visit your family. But I've been wrong before. When you saw me with your father, I knew you would confront him. Did he tell you a funny story about why we were together?" He flicked his wand. "How can you trust him when he meets with the enemy?"

Tristan didn't know what her father had revealed, and she wanted to keep it that way. With the way Tristan always toyed with her, she chose to believe her father's side of the story. If only she could shove down her fear of fighting him head-on with two mogs.

"I trust few people, but don't worry, Tristan, you'll never be one of them."

He smirked. "Heartbreaking. I see the rebellion sent its two finest to fight me."

Drool gathered in the maw of one of the mogs.

"I mean, we could just fight you. No need to bring your friends into it."

"I dislike getting dirty."

"Pity." The prospect of getting out of this alive didn't look great. The stand-off wouldn't last forever. Tristan was waiting for her to start. How nice.

"Will?" Vic whispered. "If you run, I'll hold them off."

Tristan folded his arms. "Plotting a way out? Do tell us all, Victoria."

"I said all we have to do is throw dirt on you and you'll melt. Seems pretty easy to me."

The mogs took one step forward. "That was your last joke. I really don't have all night."

"Will?" Vic whispered.

"You know I won't." He shuffled his feet, but Vic didn't dare take her eyes off the mogs to see what he was doing.

"Stubborn. First grate we see we go. Got it?" She was afraid of losing him, but his presence gave her courage.

"Yes."

Tristan raised his wand. "Show me what you've got, Glass heir."

The mogs advanced as William lifted his arm. Metal shot from his fist and met the side of the alley. Wasting no time, they charged out of the alley.

Howls erupted as the mogs sliced themselves on William's metal lines. Metal scaffolding that was attached to the building impeded the path ahead. Vic navigated through the tangle of bars, but as the mogs crashed through wooden planks, William shoved her out of the way. A board almost hit Vic in the head. It blocked their way down the street.

The metal bars shook, and William tried to bend them

over the mogs' necks, but the stone in his wand darkened and the magic ran out.

"This way!" Vic smashed the window into the storefront with the butt of her scythe. The smell of fish permeated the air. She used the staff of her scythe to swipe away the glass from the bottom of the window, and they crawled through.

A mog burst through the scaffolding and stuck its head through the window. Vic sliced its neck. Her magic surged, but this time, it didn't heat her body; it emerged around her. Before she could think about it, the mog wrenched its neck free.

Bins of iced fish crashed to the ground. The fish slid over the smooth floor, and as they ran to the back of the shop, their feet slipped on the ice. Vic took William's hand to steady them. The store grew darker the farther they went inside. The sounds of the mog hurtling through the fish displays urged them forward.

Vic ran into a counter, and William barreled into her. "Ouch!"

They scrambled, and Vic turned to see the mogs' glowing eyes. The other one had made it into the store.

They inched along the counter as the mogs skulked toward them. A loose glass case was in her path. Vic squinted as her eyes adjusted to the light, and she found a floor-to-ceiling tank filled with water and a couple of grinning alligators. There weren't many sold in Verrin, and the price of their meat was more for founders. The gators thrashed in the tank, their eyes reflecting the bit of light from the windows.

She'd never met one outside the walls, and she was tempted to keep looking at it. Apparently, even with short legs, they were fast.

"Is that smell coming from you, Glass?"

Tristan picked his way through the broken scaffolding but stopped by the door.

If Vic let her magic go, surely she could take out one of the mogs with only a little damage to herself. Ignoring the healers' warnings, Vic lashed out at the mog in front of her, gouging its fleshy black side. Her magic burned through the air, and the mog vanished into a pile of bones. Before she could move, the other mog dove, and she sliced its side, but she wasn't its target.

In a blink, it had pounced on William. Its claws opened him from his shoulder down to his leg. William's lips opened in surprise, but nothing came out of his mouth as he collapsed.

"No!" Vic exploded with power, and her scythe burned in her hand.

The mog turned to dust.

She dropped to William's side and hoisted him onto her shoulder. He gasped for air, and his body shook. Dark stains spread over his clothing.

Vic gripped her scythe, and Tristan stood across from her. She backed up with William to the opening in the counter.

"Where are you running? I don't think he'll make it, poor boy."

Tristan lifted his wand, and the air moved unnaturally. Holding her scythe in one hand and propping William up with the other, she couldn't fight his magic.

"I'd like to stay and chat, but I need to go. Bye, Tristan." She slammed her scythe into the large tank. The glass exploded outward, and the water crested in a giant wave, hurtling the alligators and water at Tristan. Vic hauled

William out the back of the shop. She almost laughed with joy when she saw a grate next to the trash.

She put William near the grate and shoved it open. As he shook, she gripped his hands and lowered him down, but he couldn't grip the ladder and fell the rest of the way. Her heart thudded as she followed him down. He was still breathing, but it was shallow, and too much blood coated his clothes. Determination burned in her, giving her more strength to hoist him to her side. She took turn after turn in the tunnels, hoping to lose Tristan. Her only thought was to keep moving before she lost William. She couldn't lose him. He would make it. She just needed to get back to the base. His breath came in gasps, but Vic kept going. He couldn't die, not before she told him what he meant to her.

❧ 8 ❧
WILLIAM

William's consciousness faded in and out, but Vic's frantic voice jarred him.

"I don't know where we are! I don't know where we are!" Vic scrambled down the sewers, stumbling as William tried to keep some of his weight off her.

His clothing stuck to him from his own blood. It hurt so much fighting mogs. He couldn't see why reapers did this night after night. "Calm ... calm down. You can find it. Just think," he mumbled. He wasn't sure if any words had actually come out.

His feet dragged and caught in a crevice in the sewer. They tumbled to the ground. William grimaced and flopped to the side to get off Vic.

"Will, we need to move. We need to move."

He blinked slowly and touched her panicked face above him. "It's okay. Go ahead. I'll be fine." He didn't like seeing fear in her eyes. It wasn't like her to be so afraid.

"I'm not leaving you. You're strong. Push, William! You can't leave me behind."

His arm felt like it weighed a million pounds, but he curled a red strand of hair around his heavy fingers. "It's okay. You're my fire girl. I can go."

Her face tightened. "You won't let me give up, so you better fight too. Blight take you!"

She held his face, and her lips crashed down on his. His eyes shot open as her soft lips caressed his. She was warmth and fire piled into one. Burning and comforting. Fierceness and softness. Everything that she was grew into his soul. He pulled her face in closer, relishing her soft skin against his fingers. The kiss was everything he'd imagined, besides the fact he was dying.

She broke off the kiss and glared down at him. "Get off your ass, Sally Sunshine."

His breath stolen, he nodded, and she draped his arm over her shoulders. They limped and ran like a strange four-legged beast. His other arm held on to his ripped shirt, tied over his side wound. Coldness entered his fingertips and toes and crept up his body. He forced his legs to move. Vic was the flame that kept him moving. The pain faded, and William knew he was reaching his limit. He didn't focus on where they ran, just on the woman who held him upright.

Spots danced across his vision, and when he heard more voices, he took that as permission to pass out.

WILLIAM OPENED HIS EYES. HE WAS BACK IN HIS ROOM, WITH one light on in the corner. Samuel slept on the mat next to his, and someone was holding his hand. He shifted to see a sleeping Vic next to him. Her red hair fanned out around him as she lay curled beside his cot. His movement had woken her, and her eyelids fluttered open.

"How are you feeling?" she immediately asked. "The healers had reapers carry you up here when you were out of danger. They needed the bed."

"How long has it been?"

Vic grimaced. "A week. I've been coming up here when I'm not patrolling or catching radiant. We actually caught a few."

"That long?" William sat up too fast and groaned.

"Take it easy. The healers don't have as many tools. More and more reapers are getting caught in the crossfire of mogs or radiant teams."

Dark circles lined her eyes, and she hunched with weariness. He cautiously took her hand, and a ghost of a smile crossed her face.

"How are you handling the news your father dumped on you?"

"I guess we don't have to fight about me going radiant or mog." She touched the scar on her neck. "The gicorb blocked power? Is that why Tristan can control mogs?"

William squeezed her hand. "I don't know. Your father can't tell us too much at a time, and I doubt Tristan will be a fount of information. How did the other reapers react when you told them?"

Vic snorted. "Most don't believe me. For now, I'm the test subject. It's been over two weeks since I lost my orb. By now, my neck should be itching. They want to lock me up when Kai can't be with me, but he refuses. They also want to relocate because they don't trust my father anymore."

"So, they're taking the news that your father's thousands

of years old, a reaper, a body snatcher, and can't get infected pretty good. Did I miss anything?"

Vic pointed to Samuel. "And your brother's still in there."

"Did Bomrosy make any progress?"

Vic shifted to put her head on his shoulder. "No, but she invented some new swear words."

"And us?"

Vic nudged him. "We are engaged, after all. It would be nice to be around you after the revolution. You?" Her green eyes studied him, and her face was tentative like she was worried he'd reject her. As if he ever could.

For the first time in forever, William let the tendrils of happiness settle inside him. "I'd like that." With his other hand, he tilted up her chin and softly brushed his lips against hers. "After the revolution."

Vic put her head back down on his shoulder, and they enjoyed the quiet moment. He'd never dared to hope that on day he would hold her in his arms. She'd come to him night after night. He gently pressed his lips against her flaming hair. William might not feel like the most powerful person at the base, but he would make sure she survived.

9

VIC

Vic would rather face Tristan and his freaky mogs again than sit through another meeting with the commanders. They sat around a long table in a room the size of the workshop. The get-along attitude had fallen apart after another week of reapers getting captured or injured. The patrols of mogs and radiant were overwhelming them. In the beginning, the Orders had sat mixed, but they'd separated into different sides and corners of the table, each Order bringing in another reaper from time to time, gaining more support. Vic thought it might be better to limit the groups to four or five; Nyx already had the smallest number of reapers.

"We need to strike them down before they pick us off one by one." Becks slammed her hand on the table. "This isn't a life down here. It's been over two weeks, and if we can't charge our imbs, we won't have food or healers. We're losing excellent fighters daily. One fight to end it all, them or us."

The other seconds and commanders murmured. Vic thought Becks had a point. They weren't living down here, and when it got into the rainy season, they could be flooded out with feces up to their eyeballs. Vic shuddered at the thought. GicCorp was winning with the high ground.

"Should we wait until the swamp mission returns?" the Boreus second, Henry, asked.

Landon spoke, "We don't know if they're still alive."

Vic knew Landon was being realistic, but a sharp pang entered her chest at the thought of Ivy and Freddie. They were strong. She needed to believe they could make it back.

"At least we know they don't need to charge," Landon added.

When Vic had told the commanders, she'd never thought Landon would be on her side. He'd never liked the founders, or Vic by association.

"According to her," the Boreus commander, Gaven, sneered.

Kai cut in, "It's been almost three weeks. Do you see any signs?"

"Cut her and see if you drain blight," Gaven said. "I find it hard to believe that in all these years we've never drained a reaper."

The commanders and reapers paused, as if digging through their memories of all the people they'd drained from blight. Vic tried to think as well. It had never crossed her mind; she saw people with blight, and she drained them. Even as a freelancer, she'd used her credits to charge rather than eat. She moaned internally. All those times, she could've had a meal.

Kai spoke again, "I haven't been charging either. A severe itch is the only thing I've felt." He smiled sheepishly. "I do admit I'm nervous to cut out my orb, but I don't see the point of having it if they can control us through it."

Becks touched her neck below her reaper brand. "Maybe that's how they're taking the reapers. No one comes back from those patrols, so we thought they were dead, but they could be taking them."

A solemnness entered the room.

"All we can do is tell the reapers. We wanted to wait to see what happened to Vic, but they should make their own choices." Kai pulled out a blade. "I'm ready to go all in. I'd rather go down fighting than lose control." He gave Vic the knife.

"Are you sure?" she asked. Their entire existence had changed, but it might give them an edge against GicCorp.

"Be gentle with me," Kai teased.

This was probably a job for a healer, but Kai was making a point to the commanders. With light pressure, she broke the skin on his neck. He didn't breathe or swallow. Then she pressed on top of the orb. It popped out of his neck and landed on the stone floor with a tiny plink.

Covering the bleeding wound with his shirt, Kai picked up the orb and studied it. "I'll give this to Bomrosy. She might want one."

"I'll cut mine out when I talk to my reapers tonight." Becks nodded. "But it doesn't solve our problem of taking the fight to GicCorp. This might give us a chance to find the taken reapers too."

The meeting burst out with the pros and cons of attacking GicCorp. With a final vote, they decided to attack. Vic felt settled. This was right. Having a plan made her feel more secure. Each patrol that didn't return was a blow to morale, and they needed to take action.

Gaven rubbed his face. "We need to figure out how to get into Haven and GicCorp."

Vic raised her hand. "I might have an idea."

Every head turned to her. She avoided talking at meetings since she mostly brought shocking news they would have to deal with. But at the mention of infiltrating Haven and GicCorp, Vic had remembered her sister's vital ceremony.

"Can we pretend to be radiant and follow them? We've captured enough radiant, so we know what they wear. We could snag a few from formation and replace them with our own people. The hardest part will be taking down the originator who gives the orders."

Silence greeted her.

Becks was the first to speak. "That might be crazy enough to work. Even better if we can get one of the hooded figures. Then we'd only need to keep one radiant to show us the way back. That would give us six reapers to gather information."

"The only danger will be for the person in the hood. They won't get away with smiling and blank eyes," Gaven added. He shifted to look at Vic. "Doesn't your radiant friend have two purified ones he can order around?"

"Yes?" Vic had a strange feeling.

"Instead of sending in reapers, can't he order them to follow the hooded figure until they find out how to get inside? Then they can come back or unlock the door for us?"

Vic twisted the ring on her hand. "It might be difficult giving them so many instructions." She took a deep breath. "Also, Sam and Xiona were forcibly purified. The reason we're capturing radiant is to protect them since they're only fighting us because they have no choice. I'd like to think we're better than GicCorp."

Gaven nodded. "You're right. I was just looking at all the options."

The others in the room nodded too. Vic was relieved that they didn't want to go through with that plan.

"I gladly volunteer for one of the spots," Vic offered.

Kai stopped Landon from raising his hand. "I should go. I want you to lead Nyx if something happens to me."

Vic cringed. Kai was doing the right thing by keeping Landon behind. The Nyx reapers still trusted him more than Kai.

"I'll go too. My second will stay," Becks stated.

The Boreus second, Henry, volunteered to go too.

"Before we fill any more spots, we should offer the post to Bomrosy, if she wants," Kai said. "If we run into something, it might help to have her with us, and we can ask William too since he knows the most about how radiant act, and he's also an imb."

Becks replied, "Ask them after the meeting is out. Then we can go find clothing from the captured radiant that fits. We'll need a team to take on the group and capture them all so we can infiltrate GicCorp."

With that, they planned which route they would take. The reapers would go in as a small army to take down the group as quickly as possible. They wanted to go near morning so they wouldn't have to patrol as fake radiant all night. From scouting, they already knew what time the radiant patrols returned, and they had clothing from the radiant they'd captured.

When the meeting ended, Vic and Kai left to go ask Bomrosy and William if they would join them.

They entered the workshop, and Bomrosy was bent over

her workbench, with William imbuing metal into various shapes next to her.

"I don't think that works. We need something that can hold it in." They turned at the sound of Kai and Vic coming inside.

"How'd the meeting go?" Bomrosy asked, turning back to her tools.

"We wanted to ask if you two would be up to infiltrating GicCorp?"

Bomrosy dropped her tools. "Blight. Is this a new death mission?"

Vic picked up a thin piece of metal that William had made. "I hope not. We might find something that can help. We thought it would be good to have you with us. And William knows how radiant act and how the orders given to radiant work."

William put down his wand and stretched out his hands. "It might be good that I help, then."

Bomrosy let out a puff of air. "I guess it makes sense. But if I'm gone, no one will understand where I left off in my research about the radiant. Everyone is more dependent on magic."

"If we run into trouble, we can ditch everyone, and I'll save you," Vic replied and put the metal back on the table. She looked at the stones and rings. Bomrosy was right. None of it made sense to her.

"When do we leave?" Bomrosy asked.

"Tonight."

VIC FIDGETED AS SHE WAITED UNDER THE SEWER GRATE WITH the other reapers dressed in red uniforms.

"Better get it all out now." Bomrosy patted down her top. "Can you see my tools?"

Vic studied her friend. "No. Your tools will be easier to hide than our scythes." It had taken many adjustments for the reapers to be able to put their scythes under the tops. At least the clothing was loose. Kai wasn't dressed yet since they'd voted that he should be the hooded figure; he had the stature and confidence to fake it, or so they hoped.

Vic's red hair was tied back, and they'd done their best to dye it dark brown. She wiped the sweat off her neck, and her hand had some brown dye on it.

Bomrosy flicked Vic's hand. "Careful. It took a long time to cover up the brands. Don't touch anything."

A hand clasped hers, and she looked up at William. "It's rare to see you nervous."

She smiled weakly. "I'm worried about what else we'll uncover. I'm not sure my brain can take it."

William squeezed her hand. "I'll be right there with you. I mean, if Tristan ripped off his face to show he was a mog all along, would we even be surprised?"

"He does look like one," Vic added.

"It's the teeth. His parents must not have taught him to brush."

She laughed quietly. The grate opened, and bodies thudded to the ground. The hooded person was out cold, and one by one, the reapers retreated underground.

"Quick, take off their clothes."

If Vic had been expecting a big revelation upon seeing the hooded figure's face, it didn't happen. The man looked like anyone else, with brown hair, a thick beard, and a medium build. It wasn't like she'd had a picture in her mind of what a body snatcher would look like. He looked normal, just like her father. If something went around that was a thousand years old and killed people's souls, she would have pictured something more like mogs. She'd never seen him before, so he had to be one of the people waiting for the body's family to die out. A morbid thought.

They made quick work of stripping the uniform off the man, leaving him in his undergarments.

Becks nudged the leader with her foot. "I'm not sure I want to take him to the base. If he gets loose or can be tracked, GicCorp could find us."

Kai adjusted the hood over his head. "I agree. We need to tie him up and leave him in a building. Take the radiant back with you, and we'll shove him in a store."

They would need to make it out of GicCorp before anyone found him. Five radiant went with the other reapers, but they kept one. He struggled in the reaper's hold. The reapers had attacked fast, before the hooded man could order the radiant to fight back, but holding the radiant was causing him to disobey his order to patrol. He struggled in the reaper's arms, trying to return to the streets above the sewers.

One by one, they climbed out of the sewers. William had explained that radiant were given standing orders, such as to patrol or return. Attacking was based on who they saw. Even though most Verrin citizens would be off the streets, the originators wouldn't tell the radiant to attack unless they saw that they were reapers.

After what felt like hours, the radiant turned onto the main road and marched. Vic's group rushed to keep in step. The hardest part was staying in a line. Vic sweated in the humid air, and her stray hairs clung to her neck. She didn't dare move her hand to fix anything. Of course she had a horrible itch that was growing worse the closer they got to GicCorp.

The outer stone walls towered over them as they passed through. The radiant went to the main gate. Off to the side, there were different sections that dealt with charging stations and managing the lines. Without hesitation, the radiant walked past all the quiet buildings. The blight in the sky swirled a light pink as the sun rose.

Vic's stomach sank as more radiant teams joined them. The hooded leaders didn't wave or acknowledge one another, but they all got into place and marched inside the walls where no one but the Nordics and, she guessed, the other body snatchers went.

The urge to scratch her itch plagued her as she marched in step with the radiant. Then the other radiant branched off from the hooded figures. She kept marching and didn't look back as they left Kai alone. The radiant formed into lines of two, then went into separate rooms. The left line went into a large room on the left, and her line went to a room on the right. Becks, Bomrosy, and Henry ended up on the left, and she and William on the right.

In a matter of minutes, they were divided into three groups. No hooded figures were in the room, which was long and wide and filled with cots. Vic didn't want to chance looking around too much. They passed a row of communal toilets and sinks. The radiant cleaned themselves with mechanical motions. Vic found an empty corner, and William followed her.

"They aren't marching?"

He whispered, "They likely have standing instructions.

Once you give radiant a task, they complete it. So, something like, 'After patrol, clean up and go to bed.'"

"Will they notice us not doing it?"

"Unless they have an order to notice a strange radiant, no. From the reaper recon, they only attack when given a specific order at that time, so it must not be a standing order." William held his wand in his sleeve.

"There's so many." It was overwhelming to see so many people. Had their families given up on them coming back? Did they think they'd been eaten by a mog?

William brushed his fingers against her hand. "We should keep going."

Vic finally scratched her side with a sigh. As she tried to brush out the wrinkles in the clothes, a familiar flash of black hair caught her eye. Vic dashed forward and grabbed onto the radiant. It was Maddox.

"No," Vic gasped.

Maddox smiled at her, her eyes blank.

"No, no, no." An arm went around her, and Vic's eyes blurred with tears. "It's my fault she's here."

"No, it's her father's fault."

"Can we take her with us?" The thought of leaving her behind again hurt.

William put out his hand. "Come with us."

Maddox didn't listen but tried to tug out of Vic's grasp.

When William met Vic's eyes, she knew. "The one who purified her has to change the standing order?"

"Only they can change it. She'll fight us if we try to take her."

A tear ran down Vic's face as she let go. "She doesn't know how to fight." Was she forced to take on reapers every night? If Maddox got killed, could Vic blame the reaper for defending themselves? Did Maddox see everything she did?

"We'll fix this."

Vic took a deep breath to calm herself as she watched her old friend lie down on a cot. It wasn't easy to turn her back and go to the door, but William's hand kept her steady. They peered out and met the eyes of their other group members. Becks motioned for them to go out.

The hall was clear, but there were no significant marks on the walls. The lights glowed in the distance, showing more wall. The group walked quickly down the hall. The radiant rooms were so large it would take a bit to reach the end.

The path forked, and Vic worried Becks would want to separate, but she signaled to go right.

"The left path should go out to the walls, and we need to find where the originators are staying."

Everyone followed, Vic walking between Bomrosy and William. She looked at her friend, and Bomrosy's face remained calm.

"You doing okay?"

"I haven't fought in a long time, but I am curious about what we'll find."

The paths forked, but Becks stayed on the main path. They glanced into empty rooms and down halls that all looked similar. They didn't have much time, but if some of the reapers weren't purified, they wanted to find them.

A thrumming brushed against her skin. The reapers paused, and William raised his brow in question.

"You all feel that?" Vic asked

Becks frowned. "It feels like magic. Like I'm using my scythe."

They all nodded.

"Do we follow it?"

The thrum of magic intensified as they walked. It didn't feel uncomfortable, but mostly powerful. Vic splayed her fingers like she wanted to hold the power. It was in the air but still distant, like it was from a relict that wasn't theirs.

A reddish light stretched out into the hall, and they slowed their pace as they approached. There were no guards down here. Tristan and his group must feel like they didn't need guards this deep inside.

The light shone through an empty doorway.

They glanced at one another and entered the room. Red light coated the walls. A large smooth dome with metal braces ran along the edges. There were at least ten other open doorways. More metal arched along the walls and met in the center. In the metal braces, stones pulsed brightly at intervals. Across the floor, the metal ran to the center of the room. Vic narrowed her eyes at the structure in the middle.

William stopped walking. "Are those ..."

Vic bit her lip. "They're scythes."

"How many are there?" Henry asked.

Bomrosy got closer, and the rest followed behind her. "About fifty?" She walked around the center, speaking to herself. "They're connected to the metal running up the walls, and those stones are generating magic too. There's an opening at the top, but I can't see past it."

"Don't touch anything," Becks cautioned.

"I won't, but there's something behind the scythes. Some sort of containers? Most look empty, but some of them are full."

Becks leaned in. "What are they doing down here? Who do these belong to?"

Vic exchanged a look with William. "The body snatchers?"

"From what your father said, it makes sense. If they're reapers, these must be their relics." William stayed back as all the reapers went to take a closer look.

Vic eyed the glowing stones on the scythes. "There aren't any gicgauges."

Bomrosy got so close her nose almost touched them. "Either they're getting drained immediately, or gauges aren't needed."

Vic brushed her scythe with her fingers through her clothing. She'd almost died when she'd used her scythe without the gauge in Haven. "Maybe they're doing something that doesn't need as much power." She thought about her last fight and how the magic had worked around her instead of through her. Maybe without the orb, the magic didn't need to burn through her body.

Becks rubbed her hands along her arms. "It feels like a lot of power. It has an odd call to it, like I can and can't use it at the same time."

Vic felt it too, and it connected to her with her scythe. The pull to the other scythes thrummed in her mind. She calmed her breathing. William approached her, his mouth moving, but she couldn't hear what he was saying. A burn crept up her hands, reminder her of the magical fire. The magic called to her. Red filled her eyes, and she tasted blood in her mouth. Someone pulled her hand, but she reached out to touch the power again.

Screams. Agony. Fear.

Vic choked on the blood filling her mouth. Her throat was raw. In her head, wails echoed and pounded against her skull. They wanted out. She felt their pain but couldn't reach them.

A slap jarred her, and she looked up into Becks's eyes. "What part of no touching didn't you understand, Glass?"

Vic doubled over, shaking. The wailing in her mind blocked out her own words. She wanted to scream with them. A clean linen scent filled her nose as William held her. Her hands covered her ears. Wetness coated her face, and she didn't know if tears or blood was coming from her eyes.

"She's bleeding!"

"Find something interesting?"

They all turned around and froze. Tristan stood across the room, with other hooded figures behind him. All of them had their wands drawn.

"Go!" Beck ran for the door.

William yanked Vic to her feet, and she stumbled. Her feet wanted her to go back to the voices. In her muddled thoughts, she knew she needed to run, but her body wanted to collapse. Becks and Bomrosy made it through the door, and as Henry approached, a stone wall formed. He dove to get through, but it crushed him, and his screams faded as he died. Vic choked back vomit as she and William almost ran into Henry's lower half, his legs twitching. William took a sharp turn, pulling her. One by one, the doors filled with rock.

"Will?" Vic rasped. Her legs felt like they were in mud.

He pulled out his wand, his jaw set. The metal from the wall bent into the doorway, blocking the stone and leaving them a tiny gap. William forced his body through, but she got stuck as the rock climbed and pinched her at the waist.

She gripped his arms, and as he tugged, her arms weakened. Her scythe harness got caught in the rocks, and she fumbled with the clasp.

"Take it off!"

"I'm trying!"

Stone crept down from above, and voices came from behind.

He put his hands under her armpits and pulled. She yelled in pain as they gripped her from the other side by her ankles. She kicked, and someone yelped. She continued to flail her feet as William yanked on her body.

Something gave, and she tumbled to the ground on top of him. He shoved himself up and helped her to her feet. Not knowing where they were going, they ran down the hall. She kept stumbling over nothing. Her sight blurred in the dark halls. So much pain coursed through her.

"Let me carry you."

Nodding, Vic climbed onto his back. She buried her face in his neck as he ran. She wanted the voices out of her head. Their voices faded, but her body throbbed. She was getting blood all over William.

The others had taken the path they'd followed inside, and Vic worried they could be trapped in this maze forever.

"We should turn off so they won't see us when they come after us." William panted as he ran.

"You should leave me."

"Not happening."

He turned left, which might lead them outside if they hadn't gotten turned around too much. The pull of magic lessened, so they were getting farther away from the central room. Her head cleared, but her body felt cooked. They needed to get above ground to get their bearings.

"Look for stairs."

William didn't respond but kept running. She hoped he'd be okay since he seldom ran and he had her on his back. With the threat of death, the body just kept going.

To the right, stairs ran upward. If they got to the main floor, they would have more doors out into the city. The sun would be up by now, so Tristan couldn't come after them with mogs.

She heard shouting, and William slammed a door open

into a room. After making sure it was empty, he placed her down and shut the door. They leaned against it and waited until the yelling had passed.

Her eyes adjusted to the room. A tiny window let in enough light to see that it was filled with storage. William helped her up and pulled her behind the shelves to the back. Sacks and boxes had been tossed in here to be forgotten. In the corner of the room, Vic sat on a crate and William next to her. They couldn't see the door from behind a shelf filled with candles.

"Why do they need all those?" William asked.

Vic studied the candles, short, tall, used, and new. "Hopefully not in a human sacrifice ritual." Her voice still sounded raw, and she would have faced a mog right now for a cup of water.

She'd meant to be funny, but neither of them laughed. What if they had human sacrifices? Her father had never explained how they transplanted a soul from one body to the next.

William leaned against the wall and pushed back a loose board poking him in the arm. "I'll have nightmare fuel for days. What happened to you back there?"

Vic rested against him, and he wrapped his arms around her. "There aren't many first-generation scythes anymore. They were calling to me and my scythe." Vic swallowed. "When I touched it, I heard people screaming. They were in so much pain. They were so afraid." Her eyes burned with tears.

William took a corner of his shirt and wiped the drying blood from her face.

"What do you think that was?"

"I don't know. Maybe it has to do with souls. Maybe that's how they keep their souls and move them to fresh bodies."

Vic shifted and pulled out her scythe. "None of theirs had a gauge either. Do you think mine will be more powerful now? Can it move souls from body to body?"

The scythe caught the light, and the stone gleamed. Touching it made it hum with magic.

"We need to talk to your father again. If we wreck that room down there, would that take away some of their power?"

Vic hugged her scythe to her. "You're right. I need to talk to him. It's strange. I don't know who my actual father is. He stole someone's body, and that's horrible, but if he hadn't taken the body, it wouldn't be him." Wasn't it right to hope that the person got their body back? "If I didn't have father issues before, I definitely have more than my fair share now."

William held up a nail from the floor and used his wand to twist it. "Remember the room with all the burned-out stones and twisted metal?"

"Yes?"

"That might have been their first room."

Vic thought back to the piles of junk. The room was a large dome too. "They moved it?"

"The stones burned out."

"They must have figured out a way to keep the stones working. They aren't with the scythes, so what are they using to power all the metal and stones, and why does it need to be powered up?"

William rested his head back and sighed. "The more we think about it, the more confusing it gets. And your father will only last a minute if we ask."

"We should ask what that room does."

"The lines on the floor of the room match the ones that carry blight. It's the same shape, but I wouldn't know if it was blight unless I saw inside it."

"Should we try to go back or get out of here?"

"We need to leave and talk to your father, then tell the reapers anything helpful."

Vic stood, and forcing her body to remain steady, she picked her way across the room to the window. William got up too as she quietly stacked crates to reach the window.

She climbed on top and tried to look out. "It's sealed shut."

"We can't have it too easy."

Vic smiled down. "But the glass is surrounded by metal."

"Will we fit? And where does it lead?"

"The good news is that we will fit. The bad news is that we'll land in the courtyard with all the workers. It looks like a few are arriving."

Vic got back down, and William helped her step off the last crate. "We'll have to get out without being spotted before they lock the gates."

They looked at their outfits.

"This won't go over well." William stretched out the dark red fabric. "These won't match the workers' jumpsuits."

Vic pulled off her shirt, and William turned away, blushing. "I have a shirt on underneath."

"Oh."

Vic snorted. "Now I have a black shirt and red pants. We'll just need to walk with confidence. As long as we don't look like reapers, we should be fine."

"Let's hope they don't see the dried blood on your face.

We might be better off going now, before they change for work. Can you walk that far?"

"I'm going to have to."

Vic held the boxes while William climbed, and he imbued the metal around the window. After the window was loose enough, he carefully edged it outward from the frame and leaned it against the wall. William looked around and pulled himself through the window.

He waited a minute, then reached in for Vic. She let him pull her. Her arms slipped a few times, but she got out. Vic stood nonchalantly as William put the glass back over the window. He didn't bother to seal it all the way, just enough so it would stick.

They walked away slowly to avoid attention. The imbs coming to work were focused on their tasks, so no one gave them a second look.

The gate was only a few feet away when Vic heard a deep voice yell, "Hey, Bait!"

"Blight," William whispered. He made sure Vic could still lean on him as he turned to face the large woman approaching them. "Nice to see you again, Julian."

The woman could've started a bar fight and finished it. Vic tried to look friendly and normal.

"Worried about what happened to you. Are you back to work today?"

"No, my friend here got sick and had a huge nosebleed. I'm taking her home."

Julian bent her neck and took Vic in. "She doesn't look too good. Let me help you."

Without waiting for permission, Julian hoisted Vic into her arms and strode toward the water taxis.

"Uh, thanks." Vic couldn't relax in Julian's arms, and William hovered next to them, looking too suspicious.

Julian placed her down in an express taxi. "Nothing to it. Stop by and see me sometime, Bait." Vic thought she saw something behind the woman's look, but it faded quickly.

"I will."

William got in and protested as Julian used her credits. "Don't make a fuss. I'm thinking you don't have any." Again, her tone gave Vic pause. Julian knew something.

William selected the location, and the boat shot off before Vic could say anything.

"What was that about?" Vic melted into the seat. She wanted to sleep for a month.

William's gaze stayed on where they'd left Julian. "I'm not sure. We're so busy fighting underground and at night that I don't think we know what's going on with the imbs up here."

"We don't know how many will follow Tristan or the reapers." The reapers had never gotten much of a chance to build up their case. GicCorp surrounded people with the news they wanted them to have. While the reapers fought every night, the imb fought to survive too.

The boat slowed as they got to the stop near Vic's home. They could get down to the sewer from there, but they needed to question her dad about the room.

William put his arm around her waist, and they looked more like lovers than a man propping up a woman. Vic didn't mind. The memory of the screams quieted when she was near him. She searched ahead for the prism of the Glass house in the morning light. A blankness appeared on the horizon. Vic blinked and staggered forward. The Glass house had shattered.

Piles of broken glass glimmered in the blighted sun like jewels. Vic fell to her knees and extended her shaking fingers to touch a shard.

"W-where is my family?" Her face lifted.

William stared ahead with a grim expression. "We need to leave." He reached for her, but she jerked her arm out of his fingers.

"Where is my family?" Vic screamed.

People on the street scattered and ran away from her.

Panic flashed on his face. "Vic, we can't stay."

Vic cried, "No, I need to find my sister. I told her she'd be safe here. She is safe here. Safe."

Again, William pulled her away. "Please, we need to go."

Vic slammed her fists against him as he tried to wrap his arms around her. "My family's in there!"

William tightened his arms. "They aren't in there. I don't think they would have left them in there. Your family's too important to GicCorp."

Vic stopped moving. "I couldn't keep her safe. I failed her again. I'm not strong enough for this, Will."

William cupped her face in his hands. "This isn't a failure. Everyone is fighting a war, and you're doing the best you can. We'll get her back. We did it before, and we'll do it again. We'll get them all back."

Silent tears ran down her face as she let William guide her to the alley and into the sewer tunnels. Her mind and body had stopped functioning. William nodded to Janesa as she moved the glass aside. Janesa said something, but Vic didn't hear it.

William paused, looking shocked. He hurried them to the center of the room, and in the middle of the gathered crowd, Ivy and Freddie stood with triumphant smiles.

"What?"

William's face mirrored hers in shock. "Janesa said they made it back. They're about to make an announcement."

Vic stayed glued to William as they headed down. With relief, she spotted Bomrosy and Becks. Bomrosy ran up to her. Kai waved at her from next to Ivy.

Bomrosy took in their appearance. "Blight, we were about to run back in if you didn't show up here. When we lost Henry, we thought maybe you didn't make it ..."

Vic tried to push the memory of Henry's death from her mind and bit the inside of her cheeks.

Bomrosy continued. "Ivy and Freddie have been back for a while and meeting with the commanders. Kai just walked through the front door." Bomrosy rolled her eyes. "He knows where the originators live now." Bomrosy touched Vic lightly. "What happened to you?"

Vic couldn't speak after what she'd seen at her home. She looked at William.

"Her house was destroyed, and her family's missing."

Bomrosy's mouth gaped. "No!"

Vic squeezed her friend's fingers. "Let's hear what they have to say. I can't do anything now."

Bomrosy stayed next to her as they sat. The reapers quieted, and Ivy beamed down at them.

"We've been told we don't need to keep our itchy orbs in any longer." She laughed. "Would have been nice to know earlier. The itching was the main annoyance—other than mogs, of course."

The cheer in the room conflicted with Vic. Everyone was excited, but she'd just lost everything. She knew what this meant to them, but only the image of her house stayed in her mind.

Ivy practically bounced as she talked. "I don't know what this will mean for us in the long run, but there's land without blight beyond the walls!"

Silence, then a roar of cheering went up among the reapers. Vic's emotions battled. They didn't have to stay in Verrin. If she got her family, they could leave and never worry about blight again.

People shouted questions at Ivy and her team. They laughed and answered them all.

"You're telling me there isn't a swamp either?"

Ivy's lips quirked. "Nope! It was dry land. We stayed there one night, under the clear sky."

William's face turned toward her. "No blight in the sky?"

"We were only there for a few hours at night. It was dark, but we could see the moon and stars shining in the sky."

Murmurs flooded the room as the reapers talked to one another. Vic caught bits of conversations about how they could finally leave. The biggest danger would be to imbs until they got away from the blight, but the reapers could drain them along the way.

"Will?"

His face glowed with excitement. "Yes?"

"Can you take me to my room?"

Vic wanted to stay to find out more, but her head and body were heavy. He took her hand, and they plodded back to the workshop. She lay on the cot, and William stroked her hair.

"What would life be like outside of Verrin?" he asked.

"There might be other people out there with their own laws and rules." Vic wondered if it would be better or worse. "You won't have to worry if you can get Samuel back."

"And he'll see the sky without blight." William's hand paused. "We'll stay until you get your family back."

Vic's eyes grew heavy. "I think that's what the commanders will decide. If we should just leave everyone behind."

"They wouldn't do that."

She blinked. "Wouldn't they?"

"Reapers have protected this city since who knows when. I don't think they'll leave all the unrelated imbs at GicCorp's mercy."

"We don't have an army to fight them. Maybe Julian wanted to help ..." Her voice faded.

"Sleep. Kai will let us know what happened."

As William stroked her hair, Vic fell into a restless sleep. Her sister and family haunted her, and she didn't know how to help them. Their hands were always inches away from hers, and she could never reach them as they got pulled under a red wave of magic.

Vic woke to the smell of food, and she groaned as her body flashed with soreness.

"That's what you get for touching things you shouldn't." Kai's warm voice came from the workbench.

She grimaced and stretched out her muscles. "I was never good at following directions.

"Don't I know it." Kai gestured to the food. "I got you something to eat."

Vic walked barefoot across the cold stone to the bench and stuffed a piece of toast in her mouth. She ate until she was full, and Kai just watched. Vic snorted. "William told you about my family."

"He wanted to know if we were still going to face off against GicCorp." Kai's face stayed neutral. He gave nothing away while giving away everything.

"They're leaving."

"It's what the council voted on. This would save the most lives."

Vic shoved the empty dishes away. "The most reaper lives."

"We're going to get as many imbs out as possible, but it'll be tricky. We'll have to recruit during the day. William mentioned there's someone he could talk to."

"So we're just leaving the city to rot?"

Kai touched her hand that was making a fist. "I will help you get your family back. But what about this city is so great? Let the corporation have their blight. We can't face them and their army."

Vic sighed. "All those radiant, Kai. All those people."

"Who should die so we can save everyone?"

Once again, she was powerless. One person against a group of people who knew more about her magic than she ever would. People who'd lived and watched others die in Verrin for years.

"But what about the radiant?"

Kai combed his hand through his curls. "William thinks he should talk to the other radiant leaders."

The bench rattled as Vic jumped. "Is he insane?" Without waiting for Kai to answer, she stalked out of the workshop and burst into William's room. "If you go to the radiant, they'll kill you!"

Samuel's smiling face greeted her, and William dropped the shirt he was folding.

He picked up the shirt, and his eyes went over her shoulder to Kai. "That's a bit overdramatic. Radiant don't kill."

"Okay, then they'll purify you or lock you up. It's risky enough for you to talk to Julian, but to go back to your father …" Vic twisted the ring around her finger.

William put the shirt down on the bed. "I'm not talking to my father. There are other leaders. I want to tell them what my father has been doing. If they're part of it, yes, it'll be risky. But we can save some of the radiant."

She walked closer. "Fine. I'm going with you."

William tugged on a piece of her hair. "I wouldn't expect any less." His blue eyes warmed.

Kai cleared his throat, and Vic turned around. "I don't want to stay in here for this, so I'll just head out."

"Kai, I'm not leaving without my family."

Kai smiled. "I wasn't expecting you to. We're going to raid the Timber founder, and after that, we have a small group willing to go in to destroy the room you found. While we're there, we can look for your family."

"Why didn't you lead with that?" Vic folded her arms.

Kai smirked. "You were off on one of your rants. And like most missions involving GicCorp, we've been too lucky. Most of our losses have been outside GicCorp."

She walked to him and hugged him. "Thank you, Kai."

He patted her back. "Anytime, Sparks."

They broke their embrace, and his smile was somewhat sad. She understood. Maybe if things had happened differently, he would be closer to her heart, but he also wasn't what she needed in a partner. Still, it left a pang in her chest.

Kai left the room, and Vic faced William. He had a strange look on his face.

"Is something wrong?"

He pulled on his sleeves, making Vic grin. "Sometimes, I feel like I'm not strong enough for you," William mumbled. "But I don't know if I'm good enough to step aside."

Her feet moved forward, and she wrapped her arms around him. "You're forgetting the nights you comforted me while I was worried about my sister. And the fact you've always been on my side." She ran her fingers across his blue shirt. "I do admit you were an ass when we first met, but blue does suit you better." She pressed her lips softly against his. "While I raged, you were my calm. When I didn't know where to turn, you were my steady wind. Don't compare yourself to Kai because he knows how to fight. You know how to grow. You've seen the wrong in your beliefs and changed. That's the greatest strength a person can have."

His fingers brushed the side of her face, and he leaned down to meet her lips again. It wasn't a raging fire, but a slow-burning warmth that filled her. The steadiness of knowing that someone was behind you. The rock in the storm. Vic pressed her lips against his and ran her hands through his hair. With William, she finally felt at home.

A maya trailed her fingers down the luxurious cloth. The pale green dress was gorgeous, but her face pulled into a frown as she glared at her husband. "Fancy dresses won't fix the fact I'm once again stuck in a room." First, she'd stayed in that cold, ugly glass house. Now she was stuck in their room at GicCorp. "What was the point of pulling me out only to cage me?"

Tristan pulled her into his arms, and her body relaxed against him, though she refused to return the hug. He chuckled and put his hands on her shoulders. "Don't worry. You're about to be the star of the uprising."

Amaya rolled her eyes and tried not to flinch as the soul inside her raged over Tristan touching her body. She couldn't ignore the soul like the others, although she knew she only kept the soul from moving on by talking to it. Something about this one bothered Amaya, and she always wanted to respond to the stubborn soul.

"I'm so excited to be the linchpin in the uprising." She

took the dress from the rack and held it up to her body. "What's the job?"

His dimple appeared as he looked at her in the mirror. He ran his hand up and down her arms. "Our source says they will raid the Timber founder. If we make it look good, maybe your sister can save you and take you back to the hideout."

Amaya spun away from him. "Oh, isn't it annoying that your old pal found a place to hide them?" she teased. "At one point, I thought you and Conrad were more in love than we are."

Anger flickered in his ice-blue eyes. "I would find them, but it is easier this way."

She patted his cheek. Tristan had a vengeful streak, and Conrad choosing his wife over his duties as an originator had broken their bond. It also grated him that Conrad had built a hideout that had taken years. But whatever Conrad planned, he couldn't follow through. The reapers wouldn't survive long without Conrad's help.

"I'm sure, my love. I'm guessing the 'make it look good' part involves me getting injured? That doesn't sound very easy."

"Only a slight ruffling. We don't want them to get suspicious."

"The fact that they will find me at the Timber founder factory will be suspicious enough." She didn't mind playing the double-crosser, but this plan seemed rushed. The other originators had to be panicking. She had to admit the rebels had never made it this far before. The originators must have gotten too comfortable in their power.

Tristan took the dress from her and put it back on the rack. "Actually, it would make more sense to hide you outside of Haven or GicCorp. If we put you somewhere randomly, we can assume they would never find you."

She stopped herself from rolling her eyes again. "Whatever. Victoria's so blinded by her love for her sister that I won't have to stay long in the sewer."

A scream ripped through her mind. *Leave her alone!*

Amaya rubbed her temples.

"You need to control her; otherwise, you'll be in trouble."

"I know." They didn't mention the soul again since it needed to be forgotten. "Do you need to rough me up now or later?" Maybe pain would help. The idiot Conrad kept glass in his arm. Amaya shuddered. She wasn't weak. She could control it.

Tristan smoothed out his suit. "We need to deal with her parents first." There was no mercy left in Tristan's eyes. The friendship was truly broken. Love was silly that way. Conrad had thrown it all away and for what?

"Oh goodie." The screaming in her head grew louder as they walked down the halls of GicCorp. The clean white lines of the building were as perfect as always. They nodded to the other originators, some dressed in crimson from a night of patrolling for reapers. Their footsteps clacked against the floor and muffled as they went below to where their power thrummed in the earth.

Amaya felt the pull of her scythe as they got closer to Verrin's heart. Tristan had said the rebels had found their scythes. But they wouldn't know what this room did or what it meant. The originators had failed before to keep the magic burning, but this one, with their scythes in place, held Verrin together. Their magic was unstoppable, and they would live forever.

When they reached the room, Amaya sighed as her

magic caressed her. She was a reaper, always. A wand worked decently enough to let her magic flow, but any person could take it. That was what wands were made for. The true power was in the original scythes and the blood of a reaper. Amaya could feel the soul poking around her thoughts for answers. She gritted her teeth and shut down her thoughts.

In the room, Conrad and his non-originator wife were waiting. They were both strapped down to a long board so they could be propped up.

Tristan pulled his scythe from the middle, and Amaya resisted the urge. She shouldn't touch it with this soul inside her.

"Conrad, my old friend, your time's at an end." Tristan's fingers caressed the blade of the scythe. "I'd hoped you'd come to your senses, but you betrayed us, me most of all. You tried to take everything from me, so just know, I will take great pleasure in taking everything from you."

Husband and wife vented their rage from behind their gags. The woman's eyes widened. This was all new to her. Conrad might have told her something, but he was still fighting a soul and could only say so much.

"Should we start with your wife?" Tristan approached her.

The veins in his neck bulged as he screamed.

"You shouldn't have fallen for one of them. Their lives are so fleeting." In a matter of seconds, Tristan had pulled the soul out of the woman's body. It glowed a brilliant white. "Should we use it to keep you in line if we decide to let you out to play again?"

Conrad's screams never stopped from behind the gag. His green eyes burned with rage.

Amaya took an empty container, and Tristan placed the soul inside. The woman's body went limp, and soon her heart would stop.

Conrad turned to the woman he loved, and a tear leaked from his eyes as she drew her last breath. Without a soul, the body died.

Tristan clapped. "That was so moving, old friend."

No more screams came from behind the gag, the silence more frightful than his shouts.

Amaya placed the woman's soul behind the scythes. The woman should have felt honored to be among the reapers. She grabbed another empty container.

No! Leave him alone! Leave him alone.

She flinched as the soul rattled inside her.

A slow, muffled laugh came from the gagged man. Amaya stalked to him and ripped it out. "What?"

Conrad's voice was hoarse as he said, "You thought she was weak. She'll end you." A manic grin formed on his lips, and his eyes held secrets.

Amaya slapped him across the face, and he laughed as blood dribbled down his chin.

"Emilia. You can fight her. Emilia!"

Amaya doubled over as the soul bloomed inside her. Tristan yanked Conrad's soul from his body and flung it in the waiting container. The lid snapped shut. Conrad's eyes went blank, and a smile crossed his face, the original soul still trapped inside. Without further fanfare, Tristan slit the body's throat. That was how they handled rebellious souls. The soul had fought Conrad so long, only to have it end here. Pointless.

Leave my family alone! I won't let you win!

Amaya couldn't breathe. The soul was beating her back

inside the body. She screeched and met Tristan's shocked expression. "Help me!"

Tristan took the butt of his scythe and swung it at Amaya. Pain flashed in her head, but she knew no more.

❦ 13 ❦
WILLIAM

William imbued yet another length of metal and passed it to Bomrosy. His back ached from leaning over her worktable, and the wooden bench did his rear no favors. William had become Bomrosy's personal imbuer, and he was happy to help. Metal worked best for him, and that's what she needed.

After they'd raided GicCorp, Bomrosy had gone back to the twisted pile of junk and gathered as many dead stones as she could find. Sometimes, she could get them to flair with power, but she struggled to keep them connected.

"Do you need to leave soon to see your imb friend?"

"Yes, I'm meeting her for supper, then I have a meeting with a few radiant leaders." William used up the last of his magic and handed her the stone. "And that taps me out."

Bomrosy took it from him and added it to the others. She was building something that looked like a smaller version of what they'd seen in the room. She connected the metal in the same dome shape and then inserted smaller stones in the metal after William had shaped them. It was only about two feet long, but Bomrosy had an amazing memory for detail, and she'd made sure it replicated the power room as perfectly as possible. The main difference was that she only had a broken stone from a scythe to represent the source of power.

"Will you get it to turn on?"

She twisted another wire in place. "I'm actually seeing how we can turn it off. Permanently. It should be simple if we can knock out the scythes. But the stones in the arches might take a bit of work. I'd rather destroy it so they can't turn it on again."

"That would be nice. I'm going to run."

"Is Vic meeting you later?"

He got up from the bench. "She and Kai are coming with me to meet with the radiant. We figured Julian might be more comfortable with just me."

Bomrosy nodded but didn't reply. He took that as a dismissal. They worked together most days in silence, and he hoped she would one day forgive him. The only forgiveness he would likely get was after he returned Xiona to normal. He didn't blame her. He couldn't even forgive himself.

His brother got up to follow him. "Stay here." Samuel watched him go without reply. There was no activity from his brother that his father had warned him about. If anything was bound to happen, he hoped they could figure out how to bring his soul out before it did.

William tucked his wand in its harness. He didn't feel the need to hide it since only reapers were in danger. One good thing about blending into the crowd. He waved to the imb as she moved the glass aside, and he went through. He took a path away from Vic's home. He would meet Julian, the boss he'd had for one day, closer to the center of Verrin at a restaurant. The meeting should end an hour or two before nightfall, and that would give him enough time to meet with Vic and Kai.

As William walked, he thought about what Vic had said to him. He'd never seen himself as useful, more like a tool for his father. Vic might not realize that he'd changed because of her. She'd called him a steady force in her life, but to him, she was a wildfire burning up all his well-placed ideas. Even his old thoughts about his future with a woman made him cringe. Samuel had always said that wasn't him, but an act. William hoped it was true, but if he'd never met Vic, would he be out there now, purifying people against their will? That was a dark train of thought. He wanted to believe he was better than that. But would he have had the strength to stand up to his father without going through everything with her?

William climbed the ladder and peeked out from the grate. No one was in the alley, and he slipped out. The blight in the sky swirled a puckering orange. If the night sky was black, what would the day sky look like? After they got Vic's parents, Samuel would finally see the sky, hopefully as himself.

Voices rose from the streets as people did their shopping at the end of the day. He rarely went into restaurants, and excitement fluttered inside when he saw the bright sign with a cheerful fish. The fish might not be so happy if it knew what was about to happen to it.

He walked in and welcomed the cool air on his face. Spices danced in the air, and it smelled so good compared to the musty tunnels, and there were fewer spiders. Customers ate at almost every table, and it looked like the establishment could use a few more servers. Paintings of more cheerful fish decorated the walls. It wasn't hard to find Julian. She waved at him and boomed a welcome as he approached.

A menu waited for him, and Julian eyed him as he sat down.

"Don't worry about credits. This is on me."

William didn't argue. He doubted he had any credits left. He looked for the cheapest item on the menu and asked for water.

When he ordered the soup from the harried waitress, Julian shook her head. "Go ahead and add the stir-fry special to his order and two ciders." After the waitress left, she gave him a friendly slap on the arm, almost knocking the water in his hand to the floor. "I said don't worry about credits, Bait."

He took a drink and didn't rub his stinging arm. "I didn't want to be rude."

She folded her wide hands onto the table. "I guess we don't know each other that well. I've learned more about you since you left."

More guilt filled him about how he'd used her keys to break into the sewers. Had he caused her any trouble?

"Most ignore me. I'm loud, annoying, and a woman. Some can't handle it, and for some reason, they talk and do things in front of me as if I don't have ears and eyes."

Julian paused as the waitress place their food down. She took a large bite of her fish, and William followed suit.

It tasted amazing. It had been a long time since he'd eaten anything this flavorful. The imbs in the tunnels focused on growing what they needed, and spices didn't fit into that, which he understood. He did his best not to moan as he took another bite.

"You were with that Glass founder."

The food lodged in his throat, and he coughed. He glanced around the room, almost expecting the originators or, as Vic dubbed them, the body snatchers to take him away.

"Her hair was different, but I've seen her before." At his panicked face, Julian took a long drink and held up her hand. "I'm not here to turn you into GicCorp and their military force." Her voice lowered. "I'm here to help."

The food went down without choking him to death, and William studied her. She'd shown him kindness within moments of meeting him, but he couldn't make a move without speaking to the commanders. He didn't have the authority to accept her help.

She seemed to read it in his gaze. "I'm just asking for you to pass it on. My father was a reaper when he was alive, and I've always respected what he did to keep the city safe. And when something doesn't smell right, it usually means there's rot somewhere. I'm in the middle of it. The reapers are gone, and I'm working with a small group of imbs."

William could see a smidge of hopelessness in her shoulders. He knew the feeling of fighting something bigger than you. He wanted to give her hope, and with Julian working above ground, they could get imbs out too.

"There's land beyond the swamp."

Julian's fork paused midway to her mouth, and she placed it back down on the plate, her eyes wide.

"And no blight," he barely whispered.

A statue sat across from him. "How?" Her voice was the quietest he'd ever heard.

"Reapers can't get infected. A group of reapers went out to see if anything was out there. They came back after a few weeks and told us there's land and no blight."

The chair creaked as she sat back, her food forgotten. "If your leader would meet with me, I would like to join up with them. I'm guessing they have plans to leave?"

William didn't want to reveal the part about the boats, but if the commander met with them, they would have more imbs to imbue the wood. They could leave sooner. "I'll tell them you want to meet."

"Thank you, Bait. Now eat up. I'm guessing wherever you are, there isn't food like this."

They dug into their food, and he enjoyed feeling normal. The last time he'd eaten inside somewhere had been with his mother, and that hadn't gone as planned. He cleared the plate until there was nothing left and washed it down with the crisp cider.

Julian paid the bill and walked out with him. She turned her face up. "I hope we'll stand under a different sky together one day." She put her hand out, and William grasped it.

"I'm sure we will."

With that, she left him, and he watched her broad back vanish down another street. He took off at a fast clip to meet with Vic and Kai before his second meeting. He crossed over a few bridges instead of taking a water taxi. He didn't have money to waste on one, anyway. A sick feeling made him think the radiant meeting wouldn't go as well, but he had to try. Leaving purified people behind didn't sit right with him. He'd purified quite a few, so he could take them, but there were way more in the radiant part of town that were not his to command.

Vic and Kai stood in the predetermined alley, wearing clothes with actual color. William couldn't help but admire her in a navy shirt and jeans. She looked less like the world was on her shoulders when not in black.

Her face lit up when she saw him, and she pushed away from the wall. She didn't have her scythe displayed on her back, which almost looked like a limb was missing. When she hugged him, he could feel a weapon under her shirt.

"Glad you're prepared."

Vic stepped back. "Someone has to protect you. If I left you to your own devices, you might start building things naked again." She nudged him.

Kai coughed, and William's face burned. "I didn't want to get my clothes dirty."

"Uh-huh."

Kai folded his arms. "You two are into some weird foreplay."

"Okay, then, let's get going." William walked off, and they followed behind. Vic's laughter echoed in the alley, and he smiled.

They caught up to him, and they continued on in the last hour of the day. They would meet near radiant land, but William didn't want to go in in case his father was around. He couldn't be sure the other leaders hadn't told his father already. William had camped out the day before to catch one of the leaders and ask them to meet. From the look on the leader's face when William had talked to her, he didn't know if the radiant leader would show up or bring others.

They were meeting in an open area so everyone would have a path at their back. Kai jumped onto a roof and crouched so William couldn't see him from the ground. Vic stood behind him, with a wall at her back but next to a grate.

They lifted the lid so they could jump down and make a quick escape. William set up a metal bar he could close behind them to slow down any pursuers.

The area was as safe as they could make it.

The white clothing glowed in the dusky sun as five leaders approached. His father wasn't with them. It didn't mean he wasn't watching. He was glad to have Kai on the roof, keeping watch from above.

Hannah, a woman with a short bob of brown hair and tanned skin, stood apart from the group. He was glad to see that she'd come along since she was only a few years older than him.. She narrowed her eyes at Vic and faced William.

"You brought your downfall with you?"

"Aw cute, the radiant know me," Vic replied.

William brushed his fingers across his wand. "Not my downfall. I wanted to share the truth with you all before it's too late to turn back."

Hannah placed her hand over her stomach while the others remained silent, the white of their uniforms almost oppressing.

"So speak."

He took a breath to calm his nerves. "I'm not sure what you know about what happened to me, but it started when I forced purification on my brother."

Hannah exchanged looks with the radiant behind her. "Go on."

The daylight weakened as he explained about Xiona and what his father had done in Haven with the originators. How people had been stolen from their homes and turned into a forced army. Disbelief marked their faces, but they listened until he was done.

"I'm hoping you only purify people by choice. But what if I told you we can live without blight?"

Hannah's eyes narrowed so much William wondered if she could still see. "Living without blight doesn't change the meaning behind the radiant life. We will one day exist in a different state of enlightenment. Avoiding infection isn't the only reason."

The others around her nodded.

"Fine, but do you believe we should make the choice for others? Shouldn't they get to believe what they want?" William remained still as he looked from face to face. Radiant could be radical, and they only accepted their beliefs as true. If forcing someone to believe became the new normal, he feared them as much as GicCorp.

Hannah twisted the ring on her finger. "Yes, forcing people is bad, but won't that person be better off? It's regrettable, and we will look into your father's actions."

William clenched his jaw. "What about GicCorp's actions? We can leave this place and be safe from mogs. GicCorp is taking your beliefs and defiling them! You should never be fine with someone being forcibly purified. You should all be ashamed!"

Vic squeezed his shoulder lightly, calming him.

"How are we going to get all the purified radiant through the swamp?" Hannah pointed to Vic. "Let me guess, the reapers will protect us? We're safe here. We've done nothing against the city. How is it our concern what GicCorp does?"

Defeat crept across his shoulders. "GicCorp's actions aren't the radiant's fault. I just hoped you'd be as outraged as I am that the radiant are being used as a weapon. And yes, the reapers will help us, but I see I can't convince you that they aren't evil."

Hannah touched the wall of the house next to her. "This city's built on evil. Evil will end itself. If the reapers and GicCorp want to fight it out, good. Maybe they'll end each other, and we will be left in peace," she sneered.

"The purified have no choice. You should care about what GicCorp's doing to them. GicCorp is the only evil here."

"Well, that was rude."

Everyone turned to the voice that had come from behind the radiant. Tristan approached with his hands in his pockets. His ice-blue eyes sparkled with mirth.

Vic's hand on William's shoulder guided him back.

"Leaving so soon?" Tristan snapped his fingers, and radiant came out of the tunnel from behind Vic and William, cutting them off.

"Blight." Vic angled her body to see Tristan and the approaching radiant.

"I just want to talk." Tristan made a shooing motion with his hand to the radiant in white. "I suggest you leave. Let us evil people deal with each other."

Hannah didn't look back as they left. What a jerk. Vic had expected little since her talk with William had shown her colors, or was it lack of color?

"I'm thrilled to talk to you, Nordic, so can you call off your bodyguards?" The sun would set soon, and then they might have to deal with something worse than radiant. Tristan might have mogs waiting in the dark.

Tristan strode closer, his hands still in his suit pockets. His wand wasn't even out. "I thought you would want to know more about your family?"

Vic reached under her shirt for her scythe and flicked it open. "Okay, are you going to give me my family back?" She let her anger drown out her fear for them. "If not, I'm afraid we can't stay."

More radiant, dressed in red, came down the other alleys. They'd been worried about William's father and hadn't expected Tristan to bring an army. Out of the corner of her eye, she saw Kai jump down and approach William. She should've known he wouldn't run off over the roofs.

"I like taking things from you, Victoria." His quiet tone itched her skin. The old eyes glimmered in the dark. "Out of all the rebellions I've dealt with, I have to admit, you've been the most annoying." He flashed his teeth. "And something in me just wants to crush you. Might be because of an old, old friend."

Sweat coated her palms, making the scythe slippery. She knew little about his history with her father, but she hoped Tristan would keep him alive. But like her mother had said, if Tristan hurt Conrad's family, he was hurting Conrad. "All those millennia have made you crazy, buddy. You might need to talk to someone or just go and die already."

More red radiant waited by all the exits.

He removed his hands from his pockets and brushed his fingers down his lapel. "No, you will die first. And because you've been very annoying, I will take from you. I have your family, but then I thought, what else does she care about?" Tristan's old eyes settled on William and Kai.

"No."

"I didn't say anything."

"You can't have them." Vic glanced at Kai and William, hoping they might have some idea how to get them out of here. William's hand moved to his pocket, where he kept metal to imbue. Kai's scythe was already out, but they were surrounded. Even if they could fight their way out among a few radiant, there were too many; they could just mob them. Kai's gaze flicked to the roof. Vic agreed, but they still needed to get past all the radiant. It might be easier to go through Tristan.

He smirked as though he could read her thoughts. "Go for it." He brought out his wand. "I want to make a deal."

"No, thank you."

Tristan huffed and shook his head. "You're not playing along. Listen to the deal like a good girl." He flicked his wand, and a push of air knocked them to the ground.

Vic skidded back against William. Kai bowled into a group of radiant just standing there.

"Ready to listen?"

Vic pushed herself off the ground. "Give me my family back and I won't kill you."

"No, dear. You give me one of your men and I won't kill them both."

A pack of radiant dove at Kai, and he tried to fight them off. They tossed a net over him, and Vic ran to help, but they threw a net over her and William. The more they struggled to get out, the more the net tightened. Vic's scythe blade was uncomfortably close to William. The rope cut into her skin, and they finally stilled.

Quiet footsteps approached, and Tristan looked down at her. "Which man do you want to keep? I will take good care of the other. I promise not to kill him, and I always keep my promises."

"Somehow, I'm not comforted." Vic gasped as the net cut into her neck and face.

Kai said from behind her, "Take me. Let them go."

William shifted next to her. "No, Kai. They need you more than me. I'll go."

Tristan twirled his wand in his long fingers. "It's really

cute, and I would love to see you two boys duke it out, but I want Victoria to choose."

"Vic," William whispered. "Kai has a family. Let me go. I can help your sister and parents."

Why did she keep losing those she loved? Her scythe hummed in her hands as her magic pooled inside her.

Tristan kicked her in the side, pulled out a long blade, and pressed it to the tip of William's neck. "None of that now. Tell me, or I kill him."

"Vic, it's okay if they take me," Kai called.

"Will ..." Her voice sounded broken. She trusted William. But how could she let him go? Tristan would lock him up somewhere, and she might not find him. "I'll look for you forever."

He shifted and pressed his lips to the top of her head. "I know."

"You can take William." Her voice choked.

Tristan clicked his tongue. "Ah, the new lover boy. You must not compare to her former one."

Vic expected Tristan to cut her loose, but he reached over her and put his hand on William's head.

"What are you—"

William thrashed, then his body went still. The net lifted, and she yanked out her scythe and turned to see what had happened. William's blank eyes and smiling face greeted her.

"What did you do?" Vic screamed and lunged at Tristan. Radiant blocked her way, and she tried to shove them aside.

Tristan's laugh pierced her soul. "Come, William. Follow me and don't listen to Victoria or Kai."

Vic stopped and grabbed William as he walked to Tristan. "No, Will, no. Snap out of it!"

She shook him, and he pulled his arms out of her grip. She clung to him as he struggled forward. "Will, you're in there. Please come out. Stay here. Don't follow him." She tightened her arms, her face buried in his chest.

"You aren't going back on our deal, are you?"

"Blight take you! You said you wouldn't hurt him!"

"I said I wouldn't kill him."

Vic screamed, and she felt Kai at her back. "Vic, we need to leave."

"No! I always leave. I'm always leaving everyone behind. I can't leave anymore. I can fight him. William's in there. He can come out."

"Vic, there's nothing you can do. We can get him later."

Vic breathed in and choked. "No." She unhooked her arms and shook Kai off. She pressed her hands to William's face and forced him to look her in the eye. "William, come back. You're in there. Come back to me."

Nothing but a small smile. No spark left in his eyes. He didn't see her.

"Come back!" Her throat burned, and tears ran down her face. Her fingers dug into William's cheeks, and he continued to smile.

Kai pulled her back and locked her in his arms as she yelled after William. He turned to follow Tristan. Her gaze stayed on him until he disappeared. She stumbled as Kai pulled her after him down into the sewers.

Her eyes stung from the fumes and her tears. Kai didn't say anything as she walked behind him. She paused and threw up in the tunnels. She wiped her mouth with her hand and kept moving until they were back at the base. She stumbled up the stairs to the second floor.

She didn't know if others looked at her as she went to the

workshop. Samuel looked behind her, then went out the door.

"Sam, he's gone."

William's brother ignored her, and she curled up on her cot and held her folded scythe. She didn't know how long she'd been lying like this, but she felt someone sit on the cot.

Bomrosy stared ahead. "I'm sorry. Kai told me what happened."

"How are we going to fix this without him?" William had worked with Bomrosy with his magic.

"We'll figure it out."

"He didn't know me." William's blank expression as she'd cried made her ribs ache. She knew it hadn't been him doing it, but it hurt all the same.

Bomrosy took her hand. "He knows you. He just can't get to you." Her sad eyes went to Xiona, who ate quietly. "We'll get them back."

"I'm so tired of losing."

"Me too."

Bomrosy sat with Vic in silence. They understood what the other felt without saying anything. Vic was thankful that her friend just let her feel. She would have to pull herself up again in a matter of minutes, but for now, she could be miserable.

"Is Sam okay?"

Bomrosy shook her head. "They had to lock him up. He kept trying to get out."

Vic pushed herself up, and Bomrosy handed her toast. "You'll feel better after you eat."

"Maybe." The toast was dry, and her stomach rebelled, but it went down. She let out a heavy sigh. "What's next in this never-ending war?"

"They're meeting with William's contact. Later tonight, they're going to raid the Timber factory for wood. Kai figured you'd want in."

"Anything to keep my mind busy."

Bomrosy stood. "In that case, you can help me put together my model and bend some thin wires for me until nightfall."

Vic groaned in good humor. The two friends worked quietly through the day. Vic tried not to think about the smell of fresh linen or the warm eyes that were now empty.

❧ 15 ❧
VIC

Most of Verrin was made of stone. The second most common element was wood. The forest of the Timber founders took up a large part of the eastern edge of Verrin, right below the fields where the Dei Order had lived. The imbs imbued the trees to grow at a faster pace, then felled the trees and replanted. The Timber founders took on the initial stripping of the wood, and in their factory, the imbs shaped it into various products, which were usually water taxies and furniture.

The other trees in Verrin produced fruit and were only cut down when they became barren. This tall forest seemed darker than the sewers. The trees were packed together, waiting for the morning when they would be culled. The breeze had stopped, and Vic wished for the rustle of leaves. The quiet unnerved her. Their goal was to steal the planks in the factory that were already shaped. They'd brought in an army of reapers to haul the planks into express taxis and down into the sewers, where Julian and the imbs she'd recruited would mold them into narrow boats for their trek across the swamp.

Vic watched the black-clothed reapers break the lock on the door. They would take out the guards while the rest waited. If they raised an alarm, the others were to head back to the base. It felt like hours had gone by before the reapers came to the gates and waved in the flood of reapers.

After manually bending metal all day with Bomrosy, Vic was happy to have a task that required her whole body. Kai looked at her with concern when she joined the ranks but didn't protest.

The Timber factory didn't stick out. It was as long as four council rooms. Sawdust tickled her nose, and she tried not to sneeze. She could imagine this place filled with imbs forming wood. In the moonlight coming through the window, Vic could make out some finished tables at the end of the building. The front of the factory had all the prepared planks. That was a small blessing; it would make the haul easier. They climbed up the stack and passed down the planks to the waiting group of reapers.

She enjoyed the burning of her arms and legs as she pulled the planks and gave them to the next group, forcing her mind not to think about her family and William with Tristan. He'd said he wanted to crush her and mentioned other rebellions. She wondered if he'd meant to let that slip. He might not know what her father had told her. Maybe he'd been fishing to see what she knew. It made sense that there'd been rebellions before hers. Maybe he'd wanted her to know he'd crushed them all. That she was a fly, and even though she annoyed him, he could end her like she was nothing.

Her fingers ached as she gripped the next plank. Why

bother playing with her, then? Was he bored? If they always won, did he just want to see her squirm on the end of his hook before he snuffed her out?

She paused. "Kai?"

"Yeah?" Sweat beaded on his brow as he worked next to her.

"Do you think this rebellion is different for the body snatchers and that they aren't sure how it will end this time?"

Kai grunted as he pushed a plank down. "We would have to know what's different. It might have something to do with your father. Maybe he threw him off and you did too. Tristan wants you to give up."

"Why doesn't he just kill me?"

"I'm not sure."

It made little sense, unless Tristan needed her alive. Then why take William and not her? It felt like a game. He was playing for his entertainment, and she was playing for her life. Tristan and the others felt indestructible. Could their overconfidence be their downfall?

Reapers took the plank, and Vic and Kai hopped down from the stack of wood. On her way out, she noticed the unconscious guard and body snatcher tied up on the ground.

"Why would they have them guarding the wood?"

Kai followed her gaze. "That is odd. Normally, they just employ imbs."

Vic walked up to the body snatcher. "Do you think they're hiding something here?"

Kai glanced at the last of the reapers leaving through the gate. "I can't think of what they would keep here, unless now that we've broken into their stronghold twice, they're putting things among loyal founders."

"I'm going to look inside real quick." Vic jogged back into the factory, and Kai followed close behind. Instead of going to the back, she headed to the founders' office space. She remembered it from one of the many founder tours they'd taken in school as part of the "what kind of imb do you want to be one day" curriculum.

Kai appeared next to her. "Do you think this is wise?"

"You can go back."

"Like I can leave you alone anywhere."

Vic reached the office. It was locked. She grabbed a long chisel from the factory wall to pry off the hinges. When she got to work, a muffled noise came from behind the door.

She and Kai exchanged a look before the door slammed open, hitting her in the side and throwing her against the wall. Kai sprang into action and flicked open his scythe. He jumped onto a table and slashed down at the body snatcher, who had their wand drawn.

Before more people could come out, Vic slammed the door closed against a body. She barreled into Kai's attacker, knocking him to the ground. She grabbed a two-by-four and smacked the assailant on the head. He slouched over to the side.

The door broke open again, smacking against the wall. There was only radiant to deal with. It was odd that the body snatcher had come out first.

Vic took a bag of sawdust and flung it at the radiants' faces. It didn't matter if they couldn't think. Their eyes still squinted when the dust hit their faces.

Kai jumped down from the table and shoved it at the radiant. In short work, Vic knocked them on the head, grimacing an apology to the souls trapped inside. Before they could look for rope to tie up their charges, a muffled yell came from inside the office.

Vic ran in, only to see her sister bruised and tied to a chair.

"I'll tie them up. You get your sister." Kai ran to look for more rope as Vic sliced off the ones around her sister. She pulled the gag out of her mouth, and Emilia licked her lips. Her wrists were raw from where the ropes had bitten into her skin, and her green eyes were wide.

Her voice sounded scratchy, like she hadn't had water in days. "How'd you know I was here?"

"I didn't." Vic helped her sister stand. Anger burned inside her at her sister's condition. "Why are you here? Do you know where Mom and Dad are?"

Em shook her head. "They separated us. I don't know why they kept me here."

Kai came back into the room. "We should go." His face remained neutral as he looked at Vic's sister. "Vic, can I talk to you? Alone?"

Her brow went up, but she went out of the room. "What's wrong?"

He bit his lip, looking like he didn't want to say anything. "Are you sure this isn't too convenient?"

"Are you saying my sister is working with Tristan? Never!" Her sister would never betray her. As much as Vic questioned her dad, she knew she could trust Emilia.

Kai put a finger to his lips. "Vic, what if her body isn't her own?"

The hammering of her heart made Vic sick. "I don't think so. She wasn't in Haven long enough. My father said they wait to use the bodies when no one knows them anymore. But if you're worried, I can watch her."

Kai couldn't be right, but she looked at the way the body snatcher had attacked her and how easily the radiant had gone down. It seemed like they'd known the reapers would be stealing wood tonight.

"Does this mean someone told them we'd be here?"

Kai puffed out his cheeks and let out a slow breath. "Not everyone is bound to be loyal. There's always a price. Just stay with her. We can tell Bomrosy. I'll also need to tell the commanders."

The victory at finding her sister now felt like a defeat. She went back into the room.

Emilia sat on the chair. "Is everything okay?"

"Yes. He just needed help with the last of the radiant." Vic helped her sister up. "Are you okay to walk?"

"I think so, if I lean on you."

Vic put her arm around Em's waist, and they shuffled around the bodies.

"How long have you been here?"

Em stumbled over a board that had gotten tossed in the fray. "I'm not sure. I was blindfolded, and the meals were spaced out strangely. They made us watch as they destroyed the house." Em's voice caught. "I could hear Father yelling at them to leave me alone. That's the last time I heard his voice." Tears streamed down her face. "Do you think they're okay?"

Vic patted her lightly. "I don't know. I'll find them."

Em nodded. "I'll help."

At the grate, Kai helped lower Emilia into the sewers. Besides wincing when she took a breath, she didn't comment on the smell.

"You're handling it better than I did," Vic joked.

Emilia leaned into Vic as they walked. "Complaining

won't do anything. We're going to do what we have to to get through this."

Vic didn't respond. Since Kai had voiced his concern, she didn't know how to talk to her sister. Emilia didn't seem to notice that anything was off, or maybe she was just injured and tired. She almost suggested that they should put Emilia in Kai's former home, but who would watch her there? What if something else happened? Tristan had eyes everywhere. Would her sister be mad if they locked her up, or would she understand? If she was Em, she would understand.

Before they reached the base, Vic made up her mind. "Em?"

"Yes?"

"This is going to sound strange, but we may need to lock you up for a few days to make sure you're you."

Emilia's brows rose. "Who else would I be?"

Kai waited before the glass entrance that blended in with the tunnel walls.

"Can you trust me?" Vic asked.

Her sister squeezed her hand. "I'll do whatever you need."

Relief filled Vic. Kai tilted his head, and his shoulders relaxed. As a commander and her friend, it was easier on him that she'd decided that her sister needed to be locked up until they knew she was safe.

The glass folded away, and Emilia's eyes widened. "This was father's work?"

"Yes."

Em touched the glass as they walked through. "I never mastered this kind of camouflage."

"I'm sure Father will show you when this all settles down."

Emilia dropped her hand. "I hope so."

Vic watched her sister as they took her to the healers. After that, Kai showed her to a small room that locked from the outside.

"Can I stay in here with her?" Vic asked.

He looked like he wanted to say no. "Just tonight. The other commanders won't like it until we're sure. I'll grab you both something to eat, then lock you in for the night."

Emilia sat on the cot and smiled at Kai. "Thank you."

Vic stretched out on the floor across from her sister, her back against the cold stone wall. They stared at each other until Kai came back in. He dropped off the food and a spare mat and blanket for Vic. The lock clicked into place, and they both ate in silence.

Emilia placed her empty plate aside. "It isn't too bad down here." She looked at Vic. "Does it feel awkward because you think I'm not me?"

A rueful laugh escaped Vic. "It's weird, isn't it?"

The sisters giggled. Emilia stretched out on the bed. "It's like I'm not sure how I'm supposed to be me."

Vic unfolded the mat and got in. "I'm not sure what to say in case I give something away."

"I guess we can just be together and hope for the best?"

"That sounds good."

Vic stayed awake until she heard her sister's steady breathing. Without making a noise, she got up and looked at her sister in the faint light coming in from the window in the door.

Vic scrolled through her time with Emilia since Haven, and nothing triggered any alarms. But her father never had either. The body snatchers knew what they were doing. Did they have access to the person's thoughts and memories? Vic touched a strand of her sister's hair. Was someone in there taking over? How could she stop it? If the body snatchers moved from body to body, then their souls could be removed. Vic just didn't know how.

Vic sighed and pulled her mat closer to her sister's cot. Maybe there would be a day again when she could watch her sister make her art. She fell into a restless sleep as questions plagued her mind.

V ic stood with Kai as Julian's voice boomed in the sewers. She took in the intimidating woman, a grin sneaking across her face. They were at the edge of the sewers, near a grate that opened into the swamp. The commanders didn't want to risk bringing in imbs that weren't related to the reapers into the base. They would guard the boats at night, but now that they'd started building them, they were on a timeline. The imbs worked smoothly, passing the imbued board to the next person, and each boat grew piece by piece.

Julian trudged up to Vic. "We have more imbs who can work, but it would be too obvious to bring them all down here. As long as the number of reapers doesn't change, I have in mind how many boats we'll need. This should take a week, if we can keep at it and cycle out the imbs who've used up their power."

Even though she was talking to Vic, Kai nodded. "Thank you, Julian."

She grunted and walked away.

"Is there a reason she doesn't like me?" Kai asked.

Vic bit back a grin. "Apparently, men don't listen to her."

"Oh, I'll listen. Otherwise, I have a feeling she'd crush me."

"You could always try charming her with your looks? Make use of that body?" Vic helped an imb struggling with a larger plank and set it beside where they were working. They nodded their thanks and formed the wood.

Kai folded his arms over his chest. "Make use of my body?"

"Just trying to help. It obviously hurts your delicate feelings that Julian isn't into you." Vic dusted off her hands and winked.

"I'll survive." Kai scanned the operation. "We're leaving in a week."

The loaded statement made Vic's chest clench. "I have a week to find William and my family."

"We're destroying the magic generator, or whatever Bomrosy calls it. Don't worry. We'll look until we find them."

She knew he meant those words, but she also knew it was impossible to search all of GicCorp. And what if they were being kept at another founder's home? Or even in Haven? If her sister wasn't a plant, then Tristan would find some hole in Verrin to keep her mother and father.

"I'm not leaving without them."

"I know." His face softened. "I wish I could stay."

"I don't expect you to stay behind with my family when you need to protect yours."

Reapers might be immune to blight, but imbs weren't. Mogs also lived out in the swamp. All the reapers were needed to drain imbs and fight mogs. It would take days to get beyond the blight. Ivy's team had moved faster, but their gauges had filled quickly. Bomrosy was now working on something to empty the gauges and release the blight back into the world, but she was only one person. Finding out how to reverse purification was now on the back burner. Sam was tied up in his room since he kept throwing himself at the door to break out.

"This might be an unpopular thought, and I need you to tell me if I'm being too careless."

Kai pushed the next plank to the waiting imbs. "Oh, and you'll listen to me?"

"Shut it." Vic jabbed him. "I think Sam can find William. What if I took him with us on the raid? Would that be putting him in too much danger?"

He grew pensive. "Samuel isn't eating anymore, and he lashes out at anyone who comes near him. If this goes on much longer, he could starve to death. Taking him with us ... I'm not sure the others, or even William, would like it."

"I know."

"Then we would have to wrangle two radiant. Although Samuel might calm down when we find William."

"He also might calm down when we let him out to find his brother."

"Doesn't he act weird for a radiant?"

Vic handed another plank to the waiting imb. "Yes, and he might be the key to finding William."

They kept working with the imbs. The reapers patrolled and watched out for the originators. Slowly, throughout the day, they stacked up boats along the walls. An imb would seal off the tunnel at the end of the day, hoping the originators wouldn't notice. The real danger was in information leaking out. There was no guarantee that everyone was loyal, and like Kai had said, everyone had a price.

Landon approached them and waved Kai over. From the look on Kai's face, it wasn't great news. He came back to Vic, his lips set in a grim line.

"The commanders are meeting, and you'll want to be there."

It likely had something to do with the next raid on GicCorp to destroy the scythes. Some commanders didn't want to take the risk. Vic didn't care. She would stay and attack GicCorp by herself if she needed to, although there were plenty of reapers who wanted to get at the scythes before they left. There was power in that room, and the safety a first-generation scythe offered them on the exodus they were about to undertake tempted them.

Vic walked with Kai back to the base. The commanders were gathered in the central area instead of in their meeting room. Reapers sat on benches, quietly waiting for the rest to arrive.

Bomrosy sat in front with the commanders. She twisted her braids around her fingers, and she looked nervous facing all the reapers.

Once Kai was sitting up on the platform and Vic on the benches, Becks stepped forward.

"There has been talk about canceling our mission to get the scythes in GicCorp. Some commanders feel it will draw attention to our escape and we should go as quietly as we can. Some feel we need the scythes to make the evacuation. I asked Bomrosy to talk to you about draining blight from your gicgauge."

Bomrosy stood and looked at Becks, who waved for her to go ahead. "I thought it would be a simple fix to drain the blight. I planned to just mimic the credit booth. However, the magic that pulls out the blight is lacking." Bomrosy went behind the commanders and pulled out the model of the power room that Vic hadn't noticed earlier. "The lines are connected to the power source of the scythes. I believe this room is actually taking in the blight, it pulls out the blight from the gicgauges. I've tried to mimic it, but we don't have that kind of power. I thought it wouldn't take much to drain the gicgauge, but I was wrong. Even trying to use the power of another scythe ended in disaster."

Landon asked, "You're saying we have no way of emptying our gauges once we're out in the swamp?"

"Yes."

The commanders and gathered reapers murmured.

Becks stepped up. "Thank you, Bomrosy. Now we can hear from Ivy."

Ivy was too short for everyone to see, so some in the back stood. "The commanders wanted transparency about how much blight we collected." Ivy sighed. "Our gauges were full by the time we reached the edge of the swamp. On our way back, we fought the mogs and ran from them. This time, we'll need to drain imbs as well as fight mogs. With the reapers that are left, we might take heavy losses."

Gaven stood. "I want to move my support in favor of the last raid. I thought it would bring trouble down on us before we left, and part of me still thinks it isn't wise, but I'd rather not go on a suicide mission when we leave Verrin. We have imbs to protect."

Vic wanted to roll her eyes. She could see why they were meeting out here. Becks was smart. If they'd met behind closed doors, the other commanders could have shut them down. This way, the reapers could see the evidence. She didn't care either way. For her, it wasn't about the scythes. Maybe she should care more, but the only thought in her mind was about her family and William. This was a mere ceremony for her.

"We want to put it to a vote among all the reapers. This affects you and your families. There's no judgment if you deem the mission too risky, but we want you to know that this isn't just a power trip to stick it to GicCorp. We need the scythes, and Bomrosy knows how to disconnect the power source. And I will feel better trying to help those left behind. I've protected imbs here after my mother. It doesn't sit well with me that we can't save everyone." Beck took out paper and called the reapers up for a vote.

It was a tense process. The exodus from Verrin felt near, and no one wanted to mess up their escape, but after hearing Bomrosy's and Ivy's information, they understood that one more battle on Verrin's soil was needed.

The seconds counted the votes and showed the result to Becks. She nodded grimly.

"We'll be taking volunteers to go after the scythes. I would like to have fifty reapers in case we run into trouble. This also means you might have a chance to bond with a scythe."

Vic didn't waste any time volunteering. Afterward, she went up to Emilia's room. Through the window, she saw her rubbing sand between her fingers. Her wand hadn't been on her when they'd found her. It had to be hard being away from it.

The lock clicked, and Vic walked in. "Bored?"

Her sister put the sand away. "It seems my lot in life is to be shut away."

"I'm sorry."

"They're only being cautious. I can't blame them."

Vic stared at her sister. Was it that easy to take over

someone's body? Shouldn't she have some sort of sister sense and know? "I just wanted to make sure you're okay."

Emilia held up the sand. "Don't worry. This is very entertaining."

Vic wanted to say they would be out soon, but she knew she couldn't. "I'm going down to help out. Let me know if there's anything I can do."

"I will."

She locked the door behind her, feeling unnerved. The unease crept in, and she wanted to go back and shake her sister for answers.

All she could do was wait until something revealed itself in the next few days, after the attack. If she took Emilia out of Verrin, would the truth come out? And could she handle it?

V ic could feel the nervous energy of the waiting reapers. Julian had predicted the time correctly. The boats had taken a week to build, and they were ready. They would board after the reapers' return, and this would be the last mission into GicCorp. For many reapers, it meant closure for what the corporation had put them through. Some reapers had nothing left. Others hoped to improve the lives of those left behind. And a few wanted to see if they could get their hands on a scythe. Vic was going for her family and William.

The commanders walked among them. The base was packed up and ready to move out. They'd limited Bomrosy to the tools she could take, since the boats would mostly be filled with food. They'd brought basic tools in case there wasn't magic beyond the blight. It would have been handy to have a few radiant among them to teach them how to build by hand.

Sam stood beside her. He'd calmed down once she'd told

him they were looking for William. His smile never wavered, and the reapers gave him a wide berth.

"Are you sure you don't want to put a rope around him?" Kai asked.

"It would make it worse if I tried to leash him." Vic hoped William would forgive her for this, but Sam's cheeks were sunken from the lack of food, and they'd forced water into him this week. Now that he was free, he had more life to him, whatever that meant for a radiant.

The reapers marched out with a few imbs in the lead. They wouldn't mess around in the tunnels but drill straight through with the imbs' help. These days, the tunnels were packed full of patrols.

They all carried heavy tools to knock the stones out from the arches of the power source. They didn't want to take the imbs with them to destroy it. The reapers no longer had orbs, so the originators couldn't control them.

They'd pre-dug holes as far as they could. Now they paused before the last intersection that met up with a main line under GicCorp. The imbs would run back after they'd finished, and the reapers knew radiant, originators, or mogs would be in the main line. The walls were rougher and narrower since the imbs had worked fast. Sam stayed quiet by Vic's side, and his lack of fidgeting almost made it worse while they waited. Finally, the pack moved forward as a new tunnel opened under GicCorp, and Vic felt the thrum of magic calling to her like before.

Someone shouted from the dark, "Mogs!"

The reapers sprang into action to protect the imbs. A mob of mogs moaned in the tunnel ahead of them, blocking the path.

"Team Two, take the imbs back. Team Three, with me to

guard the doors! Team One, destroy the device!"

The moan of mogs closed in as reapers rushed to their jobs. The imbs and the reapers ran out while the others went in with Bomrosy.

Vic took on a mog before it could go after the group in the power room. She pushed the magic of her scythe around her. She thought back to her fight with Tristan, and instead of trying to channel the magic through her, she pulled it from the mogs when her blade made contact.

The mog's black flesh bubbled, then turned to ash. The reapers' gauges filled too fast. She tried to focus, but the power bloomed inside her, burning her. Blood bubbled out from her mouth, and Kai knocked into her.

"Go in with Sam!" His eyes were drawn to the blood on her face.

Vic didn't want to leave the reapers, but she worried about using this magic. Sam followed her as she ran through to the door. On her way, she dusted mogs. The reapers looked at her with shock. They'd never killed a mog so fast. Something nagged at her about the mogs; it was as if the mogs were calling to her.

She ran into the room of power, with the sounds of the fight coming from outside.

The other reapers had been warned not to touch the scythes until they'd powered down the device. The call felt stronger, and Vic remembered the power inside and outside of her. It was different from when she'd faced Tristan in Haven and used her body to defeat him. She was beginning to understand how to use the magic outside of herself; it would be safer, and she had a feeling the stone in her scythe would be safe, unlike stones of other generations.

The room glowed red with power from the stones. The

reapers spaced themselves out so they could attack the arches at the same time. Sam was her shadow and didn't seem in a rush. The other reapers came in from facing the mogs but stayed by the doors. After they were done here, she and Kai would split off to look for her family and William. With all the patrols in the tunnels, they'd have a short amount of time, and she would make sure Kai left her if it took too long.

Vic waited for the signal to begin smashing the glowing stones as she held up the tool. The power caressed her like it wanted to stop them from destroying it. It was too familiar, and she wondered why. Her scythe stayed on her back. Once everyone was in place, one reaper shouted the order to begin, and they swung at the glowing stones. With each hit, the stones flashed, and clangs echoed in the domed room. It took Vic a few strikes before her stone broke free, and it turned a dull gray as it fell out of the metal. The power tremored, but she hurried on to the next one. The reapers focused on their task, getting closer to the scythes. They couldn't reach the stones in the ceiling, but Bomrosy was sure that if they cut off this part of the line, it would be enough to turn off the power and reach the scythes.

As Vic work on breaking the stones, the dome blacked out. Shouts of panic went up, and Vic heard people running and falling over each other to get to the exit. The lights blinked back on, and the reapers stared in panic at the sealed doors, including their newly made tunnel. Then a hissing sound entered the room, and a cloud of gray smoke inched toward them from the ceiling. The reapers shouted, and she and Kai found each other, but she couldn't find Sam. It didn't matter when the smoke lowered over them; they all passed out one by one, reaching for the sealed exit.

❦ 18 ❦
AMAYA

Spending her days locked in a room with nothing to do was about to make Amaya go mad. It was difficult to hear anything through the glass door. Damn Conrad and his expertise in glass. Who'd have thought the manipulation of glass would come in so handy. She'd always preferred their old ways of forcing air, if you could call it air; it still looked impressive.

She and this body's sister had done a dance all week. Vic didn't want to let anything slip, and Amaya had played the get-along card. They hadn't counted on Vic knowing about the originators, but Conrad must have caved. Give a man a few daughters and he melts. Weak. They wouldn't be inviting him back for any more cycles. Let him rot in the jar with his human wife.

The gathering of voices and Vic mentioning that she wouldn't be visiting tonight had led Amaya to believe that this was her chance to get out. If many reapers were gone, they wouldn't notice her escape. She first needed to get out of the cell.

Amaya lifted her mattress and took the brightly glowing stone from under it. It was a smaller one that they made for imbs. Without the wand to direct the magic, it would be messy, but Amaya had made something sharp that could kindly be called a knife out of the cot frame in the back. She'd snuck the stone in through her mouth. Being in this body still had benefits, seeing as they hadn't searched her everywhere.

She put the stone to the door's hinges and focused on the magic as it blasted in the room. It took her too long to loosen them. The door creaked open a sliver. She stopped it from opening farther and giving her away. She was on the upper level, which helped her. She knew an exit was close, up above. Now all she needed was to get to the exit and take care of the imb.

The door creaked painfully loudly as she pressed it open with one hand and gripped her shoddy knife with the other. No one was in the hall, and she swiftly pushed her way out and shut the door behind her. It still wouldn't close all the way, but unless someone looked closely, they wouldn't notice. She was careful to stick to the wall so no one would see her from the center of the wide domed room.

She had to give it to Conrad again. Who knew how long he had worked on the base and kept it from them. Tristan had confronted him one night in the sewers, and they'd fought. Tristan had been rescued by Conrad's daughter. The irony hadn't been lost on her husband. If Vic had been smart, she would have let him die. That's why the rebels never won. They had morals.

She made her way to the turnoff and paused before going any farther. The exit was hard to get by since the imb controlled the camouflaged glass. The stone hurt her hand as she clutched it tighter. She peeked around the turn to see the glass and the imb sitting in the room next to it, looking out into the sewer.

Amaya threw her knife against the lower part of the door. The imb came out and bent over to look at what had happened. In a flash, Amaya kicked the imb into the glass head first. Before the startled imb could recover, she gripped him around the neck and pushed her entire weight into the spots that Tristan had drilled into her during training. The imb struggled, but her weight kept him down. He passed out in a heap on the floor. She wouldn't tell Tristan that his constant drills had come in handy. The workouts had been horrible, and she'd told him she would just fight with magic.

The imb, thankfully, wasn't huge, and she tugged him under his armpits back to the room. Now she had a wand. She could use any wand but the one that belonged to this body. What a particular soul. The wand was weak, but she carved through the glass and sealed it behind her.

Now it was time to run. She needed to get to the originators before the imb raised the alarm.

The soul in her head screamed at her as she dashed through the sewers. Trying to run while quieting the soul didn't work in her favor. The soul grew louder the closer to GicCorp she got. The soul knew she was about to betray her sister.

"Shut it." Amaya gritted her teeth. Soon, she'd be stabbing herself with glass like Conrad. "It's enough that I have to run through this putrid wasteland. Just leave this body already."

I won't let you hurt her!

"Watch me."

I'll end this body before I let you.

A loud splash sounded from the sewer, and Amaya bit back a scream that would have rivaled her head partner. A mog rose from the sewage.

Perfect. She had a weak wand and a loose mog. She tapped into the wand and probed out her magic as the mog clawed its way up to the stone path. The mog didn't have an orb.

"Blight." That stupid soul might get her wish. Amaya pumped her legs and ran. The mog was too large. Where were all the patrols looking for rogue reapers?

The splatter of the mog's gait grew closer. This body was weak and didn't have the stamina from training. That's what happened when you got thrown into an uprising cycle. You didn't get your workouts in.

Pressure built up in her mind as the soul fought her for control of her limbs. Impossible. Amaya stumbled as the soul persisted. It couldn't be taking over.

The mog gained ground, and Amaya had one blast left. She spun and aimed the wand's magic at the mog's front leg. The blast of air shot her backward, and the mog's leg bent out. It crumbled. She staggered and kept running. Now she had a bit of ground.

A voice shouted ahead, and with relief, she saw a patrol. "Help!"

The person shoved their hood back. It was Ethan. She'd never been so happy to see his stupid face.

Blinking, he drew his wand, and Amaya ducked to the ground as a blast went over her head. The radiant with him surged forward and attacked the mog, slicing off appendages. Blighted skin dripped everywhere as they tore it apart. It was a gruesome sight to see.

"Your husband's been worried about you." Ethan tilted

his head and looked at her scraped-up body. "You aren't having any trouble, are you?"

Amaya brushed him off. "I was locked in a room, waiting for my moment. We better hurry and end this before they notice I've escaped."

Ethan nodded, and the radiant followed. "Gather the others," Ethan called back.

The six radiant broke off to get everyone together.

Amaya smiled. They would end the base tonight.

"Go ahead and keep screaming. It'll be over soon," Amaya murmured.

The pressure built, and sorrow filled her body, but the soul would soon learn there was nothing it could do.

Her tongue tasted like metal as she blinked her eyes open. She was in a cage that smelled like a mog had rubbed its rotted flesh all over it. The cage was large enough for ten mogs, and all the reapers were inside together. Water dripped somewhere in the cell, and everything was damp. A few stood still, staring past the metal bars. Vic stumbled up to see what they were looking at and only found blank eyes. They'd been purified. She stepped back and counted the ones standing. Twelve in total. She went over to the other reapers to make sure they were still themselves.

The other reapers groaned as she shook them awake. She found Kai in the corner, his body still bleeding from the fight. The other reapers shouted when they saw their purified allies.

"Why did they leave them in here with us?" a reaper asked.

Vic tore part of her shirt off and wrapped it around Kai. He winced.

"To show us what's coming," she answered.

The other reapers quieted.

Vic brushed her hands off. "We can't do anything about it now. Let's help the injured and come up with a plan."

With nothing else to do, they all tore up the bottom parts of their shirts to wrap up wounds. By the time they finished, they looked more ragged.

Landon stood next to Vic. "Any idea where we are?"

Vic peered out of the metal cell. "These look like the cages in Haven, but who knows."

"Our best bet is to mob anyone who comes in, but I doubt they'd be that stupid."

"If only."

Landon eyed the still reapers. One of their companions sobbed next to a radiant body. "You really think that's what they're going to do to us?"

Vic leaned tiredly against the dirty stone wall. "That or kill us."

Landon sighed. "We should've just left."

She didn't respond, and after a while, he left.

Kai patted her leg. "We'll get out of this."

"Yeah, it's not like I haven't been caged before." There was no William to save her now. And she'd lost his brother.

In the weak light, footsteps approached. Vic could make out Tristan, and behind him, smiling, was William. Then next to him was her sister.

The reapers all faced him, and he flashed his teeth in a twisted grin.

"I'm glad you could all make it. But I'm sad to say you missed out on the party in your little hideout."

The world dropped out from under Vic, her mind spinning out of control. "Em?"

Her sister's face smiled, but she didn't say anything. Kai was right. Vic fell to her knees.

Tristan walked closer and whispered through the bars, "Have I broken you yet? Do you think your father would be proud?"

"Em, please fight it. I know you can."

Her sister's face sneered. "There's nothing to fight. Your sister was weak."

Vic shook her head. "No, she isn't. She might think she is, but she isn't. She's strong, and I know she's in there." Vic looked into her eyes. "You can do it. It's your body. I believe in you." Barely a glimmer, but it was too late. Vic had seen it. "She's there."

Tristan blocked her view. "Enough of that." He calmly looked at the reapers. "Over the next few days, you'll join your purified brothers. This is the end. You are the last ones left, soon to be none." He looked down at Vic. "We're saving you for last."

He turned, and William and Emilia followed him out. Vic gripped the bars as the other reapers sat down. They had no fight left in them.

"We don't know if he's telling the truth."

"He had her sister with him. She probably showed them the way to the base."

"Do you think anyone escaped?"

The chatter quieted, and their shoulders dropped, accepting their fate.

Vic felt a hand squeeze her shoulder, and Kai met her eyes. "I'm sorry," she said. "I shouldn't have brought her—"

"There's nothing we can do about it now. We locked her up and did what we could."

But it was her fault. She hoped in vain that Tristan was lying. But why else would Emilia be with him?

More footsteps came, and the reapers shuffled nervously. Vic looked up again, and there stood Sam, with his smiling face and blank eyes, but in his hands were keys.

"There you are!"

Sam unlocked the cage. They pulled the radiant along with them as they left the tunnels. The thrum of power told them they weren't in Haven, but close to the power source. They looked at one another and ran in that direction. Maybe they could find their way out again from there. They felt the urge to get back home and see if their loved ones were there.

Sam tugged at her, drawing her forward, and they were back in the room. Something felt different. They had broken a few stones, but definitely not all of them. William's brother kept pulling her to the center as the others ran out of the tunnel that they'd gone through in the attack, which was open again.

"Sam?"

When she got to the center, the other reapers had left, and Kai stood waiting for her.

"What's going on, Sparks?"

A familiar burn filled her, and she reached for her scythe. It didn't hurt her as she took it from the center, but now that the magic flowed around her not through her, she didn't feel oppressed by the magic but welcomed by it.

"Kai, come here."

He walked to her. "We need to leave before—"

She took another one and handed it to him. His eyes widened.

"It's not hurting me."

Before she could reach for another, a moaning sound hit

her ears. Inky black skin charged through the tunnel, and mogs poured into the room.

Sam pulled her to a different tunnel, and without thinking, Vic followed, Kai not far behind. At least she had her scythe again, but they were separated from the other reapers.

"Should we be following him?"

"The other reapers don't have weapons. We need the mogs to follow us."

Sam ran surprisingly fast. He took turns in the tunnels without pause. He could be leading them to William, which might be a disaster if he was still with Tristan. To her, the tunnels all looked the same. Had GicCorp expanded them under the swamp? Sam skidded to a stop when he reached a rope ladder. The mogs were on their heels. He climbed fast, but the ladder bounced with him, and Vic couldn't see up above.

"Let's go, Sparks!"

Kai shoved her, and she tried to breathe as they climbed. Sam had pulled out a knife and was cutting the rope while they were still on it.

"Blight, Sam, wait!"

The first rope snapped, and Vic and Kai lurched to the side, clinging to the remaining rope. They'd barely reached the top when the second one snapped and fell. The first mog slashed at them. Vic flicked her scythe open, and the blade cut into its flesh, draining it in a blink. She gained confidence in her use of the magic. The more she used her scythe without the gauge, the faster the mogs disappeared. Without trying she'd turned it to ash.

The ladder had fallen, but their problems weren't over.

The mogs didn't care about the ladder. They piled onto each other and dug their claws into the rock to carry them.

Vic and Kai looked around for an exit. They couldn't see any. There was more rope, but the last place they wanted to go was down.

"There has to be a way out."

Vic met his eyes. "Maybe only for imbs."

The dark words sank into them, and Sam stood waiting like he hoped they would pull out a wand and get them out of here. She looked over the edge, and the mogs' progress was slow.

"Can you work your scythe?"

Kai held the new scythe and flicked it open. "I can feel the magic." He raised his brows. "How's that possible when I already have a scythe?"

"Maybe it's because it's one of the original scythes?" Her scythe hummed with power and heat, and this time, the magic surrounded her instead of flowing through her. When she'd touched the mogs for the first time, she'd thought she was using the scythe wrong.

"I think I can get rid of the mogs."

Kai shook his head. "No. Last time, you almost died. And you got a bloody nose in the tunnels earlier."

Vic touched his arm. "When we use the scythe through the gicgauge, we can feel the magic inside us. After using my magic a few times, it feels different. Can you tell? It's in the air. I think I can force it from the air." Even that sounded off to her. Where did the magic come from? Was it really all around them and not just in the corrupted mogs? Something in the air almost felt alive.

"I'm not sure. Maybe just try one and we'll see how it works."

Vic stood on the ledge and looked down at the mogs. Her scythe warmed in her hand. Instead of feeling the magic inside, she connected to it around her. Vic blinked and saw swirls of color in the air, then the bright red of her scythe's magic. Sweat dripped down her face as she pushed the magic through the blade and toward the mogs.

After a few seconds, it didn't feel as forced, as if she were releasing an infection in a wound. The blight was abundant in the mogs, but when her scythe's magic touched them, a joyous relief entered the air. It became easier to breathe. Kai told her to slow down, but the magic urged her forward as all the mogs burst open and turned to ash. She collapsed after they'd all disappeared, but she didn't feel like before, when her insides had been boiled alive. She only felt a tired ache, like she'd run on patrol all night.

Sweat coated her, and when she wiped under her nose, only a bit of blood came away.

Kai helped her up and steadied her against his side. He held her face in his hand, inspecting her.

"I told you only one, but as usual, you don't listen." His lips thinned into a hard line.

His hands weren't cold, but they felt that way against her skin. "It was different. Like the blight wanted to be free."

Kai dropped his hand from her face and stood to look over the edge. "I'm not sure what this means." He took in his new scythe. "You're still worn out after using too much magic, but at least blood isn't coming from your eyeballs. That was a horrifying sight."

"I imagine. I'll get better at the bleeding part so as not to offend your sensibilities too much." She tried to walk on her own. Her legs weren't much better than cooked carrots.

Sam pounded on the sealed wall with his fist, interrupting them.

Vic told him, "We don't have a wand to get through, Sam. I'm sorry."

The radiant paused for a moment before continuing.

"Either he's been here before and the walls were open, or he's lost it. Should I stop him before he hurts himself?"

Vic pulled her sweaty hair from her neck. "We need to get back to the base. Sam, we need more people to look for William. Can you come with us?"

His brother's name was the magic word. He stopped banging on the wall and waited with them. They took the spare rope, and Kai lowered Vic to the ground. The men followed.

Sam took the lead, and shrugging, Vic and Kai followed him. He knew his way around, and Vic couldn't guess where they were located. Kai let her lean on him as they walked. They moved slowly, and even though it took less than an hour, it felt like they'd been walking for days.

The broken glass doors of the base greeted them. Numbness overtook her, and she let it. They had an evacuation plan in place for a second location, but the smell of blood was thick in the air. Not everyone had made it. The reapers would have fought to let the families escape.

They shuffled through the opening, their scythes drawn. Then she looked down at the landing. Broken reaper bodies were scattered all over the room. Vic choked back a sob. In the center, the originators had piled broken scythes.

Reapers walked among the dead and gathered them to one side of the room. Vic tried to count but stopped after fifty. They'd been decimated. Kai helped her down, and she went first to Bomrosy's shop. She found her friend sobbing over Xiona's body.

Vic flew to her side and saw that Xiona was still breathing, but in quick gasps.

"S-she protected me ..." Bomrosy held her bloody hands over the wrapped wound leaking blood. "T-there aren't any more imbued bandages. They won't give them to a r-radiant."

Anger flashed in Vic. "I'll get some. Just hold tight, okay?" She willed her body to move and bumped into Sam as she stood. He held out an arm, and she took it. They walked back out, and Kai was helping reapers with the bodies. The infirmary was too small for all the wounded, and Vic could see from above that they were putting the injured on the opposite side, all in the same room. Some reapers pulled bodies out of the rooms, and Vic blinked when smaller bundles came out, wrapped in blankets.

Numbness would get her through this, but rage burned underneath. She'd known the originators were monsters, but to harm children? She would wipe every one of them out of Verrin if it took her her whole life.

She met up with Kai, his stance stiff as he worked.

"Did anyone check the evacuation point?"

"Becks sent a small group to check. They should be back soon."

"Your family?" Vic asked softly.

Kai shook his head. "Not here."

She squeezed his elbow. "That's good." She still held on to Sam. "I need to get more bandages for the wounded."

Kai eyed her arm leaning on Sam. "Are you sure you should go?"

"Someone has to, and I need to do something." Guilt ate

into her for wanting to leave the massacre. She blurred her vision on purpose to avoid seeing the mass of bodies. Only a few undamaged scythes lined the wall, with no owners to claim them.

They'd fought so hard to get out, and in a matter of hours, they'd lost most of the reapers.

"Go, then. Be careful."

Vic let Sam guide her as she stumbled out, trying not to see all the blood on the walls and pretending her boots didn't stick to the stone.

The blue light from the healers' building stood out in the night. Sam kept her upright in the dark alley. The temptation to sleep, even among the goo on the ground that was likely vomit, was in the back of Vic's mind.

"How hard can it be to rob healers?"

Sam didn't respond.

"With how chatty you were before getting purified, this certainly evens it out." She combed her hands through her hair and stood on her own. Other than the tiredness, she'd regained her strength. Looking down at her body, she frowned. "Maybe it will be better if I go in needing help?" Bomrosy needed a bandage and soon, as did many others down at the base.

Vic leaned back on Samuel and hobbled into the healers' building. They took one look at her and put her down on a bed and wheeled her back.

A healer raised her brows at Sam, then went back to Vic. "What happened?"

"Ah, magic drain."

The healer got to work briskly, lifting Vic's shirt and wrapping bandages around her middle. "It doesn't seem as bad as last time." The healer stopped short and bit her lip.

The woman recognized Vic. Dryness made her tongue stick to her mouth, and she wavered between running out of the room and staying frozen in place. She realized she'd given herself away as a reaper when she'd mentioned magic drain. How stupid could she be? She put her palms on the mattress and swung her feet over the edge. She needed to leave.

"I have someone who wants to speak with you. They're on their way."

"What?"

The healer left the room quickly and shut the door behind her.

Vic slid down from the bed, opened the cabinets, and shoved bandages inside her bag. "We need to get out of here, Sam." One thing about him being a radiant, he stayed calm in bad situations. The bandages felt nice and gave her more energy, but she didn't want to stick around to see who the healer wanted her to talk to.

They packed the bag full, and she didn't need to waste any more time. As she swung the door open, William and Sam's father stood there in the way.

"Blight." Vic reached for her scythe and flicked it open.

Their father held up his hand, showing a missing finger. "I'm not here to hurt you. I need to tell you something."

"William shared all the information I need to know." Vic held the scythe between them, keeping him at a distance. She didn't see a new ring on his finger but didn't trust that there wasn't one on his body.

That man sure had a pair on him as he inched closer and shut the door behind him. "I know you don't want to listen, but this is important."

"Yeah, and I'm sure your buddies at GicCorp are right behind you."

Sam stepped to her side, like he wanted to protect her from his father.

"No, they used me and are done with me. They gave me my life in exchange for my silence. I spent weeks searching for someone who was part of the rebellion, then I heard William met with the radiant leaders. I've also interacted with healers throughout my life. When things get too much for radiant, we still need medicine. It took some convincing, but she said she'd be on the lookout for you. I wasn't sure if you would ever appear, so there are healers in every building looking for you."

The scythe stayed up, and Vic pressed forward, almost pinning him to the wall. "Okay, nice backstory. What do you want with me?"

"I know how to reverse radiant."

Vic scowled. "How did you find this out? And why are you telling me?"

He put his hand between the blade and his neck. "Because you're the only one with a first-generation scythe, and only reapers can do it."

"Say it quick. I need to leave. I'll decide if I trust you later."

"The soul remains in the body for a time. It will fade eventually, and those radiant are already gone. But if you put another soul inside, the original soul has a chance to fight its way out. The new soul will wear down the radiant barrier so they can break through. But if another soul is never put in, the radiant wall will hold until they fade."

"You're just telling me how to body snatch." Vic pushed closer, then paused. Her father's body was fighting him, even after years. The other originators waited to use the bodies after a longer time, maybe to weaken the soul.

"How do I put a soul in a purified body?"

He shrugged. "I'm not a reaper. I just know this from being around them. And if the rebellion wins, I want you to look kindly on me and the radiant community."

The scythe flicked shut, and Vic put it in her harness. "Wow, nothing like changing sides when you get kicked off the other team."

"You do what you must to survive here. I've done many things to protect my family."

"I don't know if your sons would thank you for it."

"Perhaps not. But in the end, we will survive." With that, he left the room as quickly as he'd come.

Vic raised her brow. "Does your dad always need the last word?"

Sam, of course, didn't answer, but she walked out with no trouble. It had taken them long enough to get the bandages that she feared it might be too late for Xiona and other reapers.

She walked as fast as she could, thankful for the bandages giving her stamina a boost. In the base, the carnage remained the same, with more bodies covered in blankets off to the side. Her footstep halted by the workshop, where Bomrosy sat with a shallow-breathing Xiona.

Vic ran next to Xiona and dropped the bag next to her body, and Bomrosy shot to attention and worked with Vic to remove the torn cloth bandages and wrap the imbued ones around her. The gash in Xiona's side was large, and her skin was clammy and cold. It leaked blood, but as long as Xiona still breathed, Vic would hope. Fingers sticky from blood, she pressed the skin together as Bomrosy tightened the bandage. Instead of wrapping it, they waited until the bandage had faded, using up the magic rather quickly, then covered her with a new one, wrapping it all around her.

After they finished, Vic ran to her cot and covered Xiona with her blankets. She handed Bomrosy one more set of bandages. "I hope this will be enough. Keep her warm."

"Thank you." Bomrosy's face was streaked with tears. "Why did she do that?"

"You told me she always looked out for you. Why would now be any different?"

Bomrosy held Xiona's hand and started her vigil over the ex-commander. Vic looked at her cot with longing but went down to the main landing to help with the injured. The next few hours were spent piecing flesh together and wrapping the wounded while ignoring the mass grave.

A shout sounded from the entrance, and Vic reached for her weapon, but it was Landon.

He ran up to Becks. "Some made it out to base two. Mostly imbs."

Becks nodded, as if she'd expected that. The count of remaining reapers would be dour. Twelve from the base would likely make it and then almost thirty from the raid. The purified reapers wouldn't be any help. From over a hundred to this. The reapers had worried about draining blight from the imbs during the crossing, and now with so many dead, it might be impossible.

"We can't stay here long. They might come back to finish the job. Landon, organize transport for those who are too injured to walk. We move out within the hour with what we can take on our backs." She blinked rapidly. "Those of you who had your scythe taken during the raid, go ahead and claim one from the fallen ..." A crack in her voice was all she would give away of her emotions.

The reapers approached the remaining scythes reverently, their heads bowed. It wasn't pleasant getting a weapon from someone lying a few feet away under a blanket.

Kai was setting up wood around the bodies and dousing them with fuel. They would leave the base in a funeral pyre.

Moving like a dead woman, Vic went up to her room, then William's. She glanced around, looking for Scraps. The longer she searched, the more frantic she became. Then under a pile of clothing in William's room, a pair of judging eyes met hers.

She clutched her cat in her arms, and he meowed in frustration over being squeezed to death. "Why are you hiding in here? I thought you got tired of me and ran off, you silly cat."

His fur smelled ashy, but she'd never smelled anything so wonderful. Wiping the tears from her eyes, she grabbed a pack from William's closet, adjusted Scraps inside, and put it in front of her. His head poked out, and he continued to glare.

"I won't leave you down here again."

She went to help Bomrosy put Xiona on a cot they could carry. With the rest of the surviving reapers, they gathered at one entrance.

They all faced the bodies in silence. No words could be spoken about the loss of life. In their silence, Beck and Kai lit the bodies on fire, and they filed out as smoke filled their sanctuary.

All the reapers were on edge as they traveled to the smaller base. The cot bounced against Vic's knees with every movement, and at the slightest noise, the group would turn, scythes clicking open.

They would have to tell the others that Kai could use the scythe from the power source, but Vic wondered if there was any point. With fewer than fifty of them left, they couldn't chance another raid if they wanted to leave. They might have to make do with what they had. With his new scythe, Kai might take on the brunt of the draining anyway.

Vic didn't want to choose, but she'd always chosen Verrin over her family. She wouldn't leave them behind.

They reached base two. This place didn't have separate rooms, and the doors were made of stone, like the doors that Maddox had made in the sewers.

The door was open, and the first two reapers held out their scythes as they entered. The entire room was empty besides a few scattered blankets.

In the middle of the floor, a note waited.

Thought you could hide?

◈

SOME REAPERS FELL TO THEIR KNEES. LANDON RAN OUT THE other exit, shouting that he'd seen all the imbs only moments before. It was too much. They'd lost so many, and now those who had made it out were gone.

Vic and Bomrosy gently placed Xiona down and watched the chaos.

Becks waved her arms, shouting to quiet everyone down. It took longer than normal for them to listen. All the reapers looked defeated.

"There are no bodies, so we can hope they're still alive."

One reaper in the back, with a line of dried blood on his face, replied, "They're probably purifying them!"

Shouts and cries came up, and Vic thought now might be a good time to share the news.

"Hey!" All faces turned to her. "I don't know if this will help, but there might be some hope if they are purified." She shared with them what William's father had told her.

Another reaper scoffed. "You don't know if it will work. And who has spare souls to put into bodies? And we would need a scythe like yours."

"The originators?" Behind the scythes in the power source room, there had been jars with glowing lights.

"If we go back in there, we'll all die!"

"I'm not doing it again."

"Let's leave with those we have left and let Verrin burn."

Becks had lost control over the reapers.

"Every man for themselves. We'll get killed protecting this blighted city."

They tried to speak reason, but in a mad rush, more and more reapers left them standing in an empty room. Some took the injured with them, until only Kai, Becks, Bomrosy, Xiona, Sam, and Vic were left.

Becks sighed loudly and rubbed her head. "You can't say we didn't do our best."

"We can't give up!"

Becks patted Vic on the shoulder. "Another charge to the death isn't in me. Sorry."

Vic looked at Kai, his face a war of emotions. His sister and mother were in the hands of Tristan.

"Let's go."

There was nothing left to do but keep moving. Vic didn't

ask, only followed. Kai saw it, too. How could two reapers, two radiant, and a tech storm a corporation?

They left the sewers, took a breath of fresh air, then headed down a familiar alley to Kai's house.

He unlocked the door, and the group entered, collapsing on his furniture and floor.

Vic let Scraps out of the bag, and he went to purr on top of her lap.

Kai slid down on the floor and buried his face in his hands. "What do we do, Sparks?"

The answer stuck in her throat. What could they do? This was the end. They would just bide their time until the originators caught them or killed them.

One by one, they all fell into a fitful sleep, hoping that when the sun rose, the nightmare wouldn't be real.

21
VIC

Vic was the first to wake. It took her a moment to realize she was in Kai's old home. The memory of him giving her soup haunted her. It felt like years had passed. But had it only been months? She went to Kai's room and found some of William's clothing. She took a deep breath of the familiar scent of clean linen.

Her teeth came down on her cheeks to stop the tears. A shower would be the first thing. She could cry later. Grabbing a shirt and sweats from William's clothes, she took a hot shower, washing away blood and ash. The clothes were big on her, but they felt comfortable.

Outside of the bathroom, she could smell something cooking. Sam stood over the stove, boiling water and adding a pack of noodles.

"Go ahead and shower, Sam. I'll finish up."

He left the ladle in the pot and went to clean up. The steam carried the scent of spices through the house, and she heard movement from the living room. Vic added all the other packs of noodles into the water. In the cupboard were rice, beans, and more noodles. It wouldn't last them more than a few days. She opened the fridge. It was empty, but in another cupboard, she found some unopened cat food and smiled.

"Guess you don't have to eat rats."

Scraps tangled himself in her legs as she opened the can and put it on a plate. She wrinkled her nose at the smell of cat food mixed with spices. "We might have to put you to work fishing, Scraps."

"Probably would do better than us." Kai entered the kitchen with a towel around his shoulders, still drying off his hair. "Got to admire Sam. He showers fast and left me some hot water."

He grabbed five bowls and glasses and took them out to the table. Vic followed him with forks, and she heard the shower still running. Bomrosy waited, resting her head on her arms.

"Xiona's okay?"

"The wound's still raw, but it's sealed."

"Good."

They finished setting up their breakfast, and Bomrosy took her turn. After everyone had showered, they packed themselves in around the table, and the sounds of slurping and clinks against the bowls filled the silence. They cleaned up, and then they all sat on the furniture, looking at one another.

"Anyone have a plan?" Bomrosy asked.

Kai shrugged and rubbed the dark circles under his eyes.

"I don't know," Vic replied. "We're the only ones left to storm the castle. We might only be able to sneak in to get

Kai's family and mine out. I'm not sure if that would even go well. If they catch us, it'll leave you with the two radiant."

"The more often we go into that blighted building, the more trouble we cause. I can't leave them behind, but I'm out of ideas." Kai's defeated attitude matched the room's. "They could be anywhere. It might take years to find them without someone helping us from the inside."

"Sam might be of some help. He seems to know his way around. We could go in as radiant again."

"Yeah, we could."

The mood in the room spoke louder than their words. They were out of ideas, and it seemed like this plan had been doomed from the start. They knew they had one last shot at getting into the corporation, but unlike the other times, they might not get out. Tristan kept William and her sister close, so when Vic went after them, she would have to fight him.

"We go after Tristan during the day," Kai said.

"You reading my mind?"

"I have eyes, Sparks. When he came down to see us in the cells, he had William and Emilia. She won't be far from his side since she's one of them."

"William's father said we have to put a soul inside the radiant to free them. But since the body snatchers put their souls in new bodies, I can assume there's a way to take them out."

Kai studied his new scythe. "We might have the right tools to do this. But where are we going to find a soul that won't try to kill off the other soul inside?"

"I don't know."

"The two of us can watch the main gate and the entrance

to his house. If we get your sister, she might tell us where they're keeping all the people they didn't kill."

"My father didn't last long when the other soul fought back. If we keep talking about my sister, she might break through."

Kai nodded and placed his scythe down on the table. An uneasiness settled in. Facing Tristan during the day meant they could have problems with the law, but they wouldn't need to deal with mogs. With their new scythes, mogs weren't as big of a problem, but it was still very draining on their energy.

"Bomrosy, are you okay to keep an eye on the house? I have spare weapons just in case." Kai got up, and Bomrosy followed him to his room to sort out what she could use.

"I might do better with my hammer," Bomrosy said wryly.

Vic winced. "I almost pity the person who tries to break in."

They found hats to cover up Vic's and Kai's hair, and they put on darker glasses. Since it was summer, they wouldn't look out of place. In the loose clothing, Vic hid her scythe, and Kai followed suit. They didn't know when they would attack GicCorp, or if they could today, but they needed to be ready. Kai put a length of rope in a bag. Kidnapping resistant people would be the real challenge. Knocking them out might be their best bet.

As they went to leave, Sam followed them.

"No, stay here."

Vic opened the door, and Sam stayed close behind her. When Bomrosy tried to hold him back, Sam swung at her. She ducked and barely avoided it, but he swung again. Vic blocked it with her arm, and Kai wrapped his arms under him. They all exchanged looks.

"William said something like this could happen."

Pinned in Kai's arms, Sam smiled like always.

"Why don't we take him?" Kai said. "It might be easier. He can help us carry them back."

It didn't sit right with Vic to tie him up.

"If you think he'll be okay," he added.

"He'll be okay," Vic stated with more confidence than she felt.

Having Sam with them might make them stick out more, but after dressing him in a hat and glasses, he appeared more like a silent friend than a radiant. The group left the house and walked to the center of town to save on credits. They planted themselves in front of different shops with a view of GicCorp and the Nordic home.

Day after day, they watched the main door to GicCorp. Tristan came out often, but he was always by himself. Vic would clasp her coffee cup tightly as he got into a car or water taxi. They moved from shop to shop, waiting and spending the last of their credits on expensive drinks they didn't need, only to go home and eat rice and beans.

On the fourth day, Sam shifted in his seat, drawing their attention. He normally sat still, but now he faced the gates.

Vic lightly touched Kai as Tristan came out with Emilia on his arm and William shadowing them. Emilia donned a hat like them, and a light scarf covered her face, but Vic recognized her sister.

Tristan leaned down to whisper something in Emilia's ear, and a light giggle floated in the air to where they were sitting.

They watched them walk across the street, and then in no rush, they got up and followed them at a distance.

The trio entered a nice restaurant on the main canal. Vic and Kai paused outside.

"Is this it?" After waiting and sneaking in and out of GicCorp, would this be her last fight with Tristan?

Kai nodded darkly. "The woman inside your sister can help us find my family. Then we leave."

The mass exodus had been reduced to a few. "If we don't survive this, I just want to say, I've enjoyed our friendship."

Kai took off his glasses and tucked them away while reaching for his folded scythe. "You sure cause a lot of trouble, Sparks."

"Hey, you were right there with me." It became harder to swallow as she looked at him. "I'm just saying it's nice having you at my back."

"Same."

She took off her glasses and pulled out her scythe. With one final pause, they burst into the restaurant, silencing the entire place.

In sync, the scythes flicked open, and they faced Tristan, who sat at the back of the room with his back to the wall. He didn't even flinch at their entrance.

"It's best if everyone leaves," Tristan spoke, then took a drink from his glass.

The patrons stilled. Then in a rush, they swarmed past the two reapers and radiant.

"How long before they call the officers?" Vic whispered.

Tristan carefully wiped his mouth with a cloth napkin and stood while William and Emilia stayed seated.

"We don't want the law to come just yet," Tristan stated. "I'm glad you could join me. After you followed me for days,

I figured out what you wanted, and I was only too happy to put an end to our journey." He opened his arms wide, indicating Emilia and William. "Here are your two prizes, Victoria. Won't you come and get them?"

"Gladly." In a blink, Vic propelled herself onto a chair. Then launching off the tables, she charged straight at him. Food and dishes crashed to the ground as she leaped from table to table.

Tristan only showed a moment of surprise, but he withdrew his wand and hurled a blast of air at her.

Only a few feet from him, she angled herself to the side and landed on the ground, her blade in front of her.

"I'm disappointed that you won't face me as a reaper."

Tristan waved his wand, and the wood from the tables twisted into lengths that crept toward her legs. "Ah, if only you knew that the only power here is reaper power."

A question popped up in her brain, but she didn't have time to work it out. Her scythe sliced through the thin wood that blocked her. Kai flanked her on the right, heading straight to her sister.

Emilia pulled out a wand, and all the glass in the windows burst into shards. With a circle of her wand, they flew at them and sliced into their skin.

Vic bent her face away to cover her eyes, but the glass lost its momentum, and Emilia's face twitched. With clarity, Vic shouted, "Fight her, Em!"

Tristan lost his composure and snarled, "There's nothing you can do for her." He flung his arms out. A huge windstorm catapulted the tables at Vic and Kai, hurling them back.

Vic landed on the ground, Kai not too far away. Sam was gone. Before she could worry, Tristan launched more tables at them, and she ducked. A table careened into her side, and she let out a puff of air.

Flinching, she scrambled out from under the mass of tables. Tristan stood in the cleared-out space of the restaurant. Her sister doubled over. Worry flashed through her, but she needed to trust her sister. William still sat at the back of the room.

Tristan noticed her gaze. "He's not worth it anymore."

She swished her scythe through the air and walked toward him. "I'll decide that, thanks."

A clatter told her Kai was behind her, and she sped to the side of the room where there was a long bar. Another breeze hit her, but she put her hand down on the bar top and flew over the bar, holding her scythe. Ducking down, she ran along the bar, getting closer to Tristan before popping her head up.

With her free hand, she grabbed a bottle of whisky and launched it at Tristan. While he blocked the first bottle, she followed it with another and another. He shattered the glass before it hit him, but the liquid splashed around his feet.

"Enough!" He blasted the bar area, shattering the rest of the bottles.

Liquid coated Vic as she ducked again. Kai shouted, and Vic heard a scuffle, then another crash.

"He flies nicely."

Vic's heart sank. Slow footsteps approached her, and in the corner of her eye, she saw matches. Her hands shook as she took them. She held the box with the striking strip behind her back with her scythe and clasped a match with her free hand as she stood.

She saw Kai back at the tables, and Tristan had stopped in a puddle of alcohol.

"Did you think you'd have a better chance against me when I was alone?"

Vic took a moment to see how far Kai was from the liquid while vapors filled the room. She couldn't see Sam.

"I had to take it. I'm surprised you set this up," Vic stalled, hoping to see where Sam had run off to. Her sister stayed far away, unmoving. "Your buddy in my sister isn't doing so hot."

Tristan turned his face away, and Vic struck the match, then lit the box of matches on fire and tossed it at the puddle around Tristan, hoping the vapors would catch the flame.

She dove to the side since the vapors also surrounded her. A loud boom and a flash of heat encased the room. Burning pain inched across her skin. Vic rolled and did her best to ignore it. She crawled over the bar. Tristan was on the floor, and a patch of blood was on the wall behind him, showing where he'd smashed his head.

The wooden floor was catching fire, and the room filled with smoke. She stood over Tristan and kicked him as she held her blade to his neck. Blood trickled from his mouth, and red coated his teeth when he smiled.

"What are you grinning about?"

"Stab her."

"What?" A flash of pain lanced her side again and again. She choked and turned, falling to the ground, only to see William behind her, smiling while holding a dripping blade.

A blur of flesh tackled William to the ground, and Sam pummeled William's face.

The heat from the growing fire prickled her skin, and her blood leaked out of the wound and onto the floor. Her fingers went numb, and a pattering of footsteps and shouts entered the building.

Tristan glanced down at her but turned away as more voices filled the air.

Vic lay there, the fire growing closer, her blood mixing with broken glass and alcohol.

"Stay with me, Sparks."

Her body bloomed in pain as Kai lifted her, but she blacked out with the image of William and his blank eyes standing over her.

22

EMILIA

Emilia stopped screaming as she watched through the eyes of her own body—a body she could no longer control. As if in a nightmare, she observed her sister lying in a pool of blood, her face defeated as Emilia's body followed Tristan. Amaya's smug thoughts bounced back to her, but Emilia brushed them aside. Her sister's words had let her gather herself.

This invader's soul told her she was weak, but she couldn't shove Emilia out of her body. There was a barrier inside, and Emilia imagined a smaller version of herself inside this mind. In a flash, there she was. She looked down at her hands, and they glowed, but other than that, her imaginary body was completely normal. She didn't feel so scattered anymore.

A hammer of thoughts pounded at the barrier as the invader wondered why the screaming had stopped. It was amazing how long one could scream when they didn't need air. She needed to help her sister. Pain lanced through memories that weren't hers. They'd gone to the base and killed everyone they could find. Emilia raged, but she was only one among the monsters, and making her body trip or falter was all she could do.

In her mind, she paced the barrier that had formed after they'd purified her. It was see-through but solid. She touched the bottom of the wall, and it was like she could feel herself beyond it. If she got past this wall, she could take on the invader. Even though she was locked back here, the longer she stayed, the more her soul faded. Amaya's soul, though, was almost shredded in appearance, damaged from who knew what. Thoughts leaked through, and Emilia found out the story behind them and just how old they were.

She pushed into the wall, and her fingers bent, trying to get a grip. The wall moved and bent with her, not letting her dig in. Emilia tried and tried to grasp it, then sat down in her mind prison with a sob. This was her body. Shouldn't she have more control over it than Amaya?

"Give up and leave. There's nothing you can do."

Emilia had grown up knowing she would go to Haven and be away from her family. She'd done it to protect them. She'd given up everything over lies that GicCorp spread so it could steal bodies and use them as its own. She'd had enough of their lies. She'd seen them kill reapers as they protected those who fled. She'd stood by and watched them cut down children like they meant nothing. They thought they could live forever, and they'd crushed a thousand rebellions. They'd done it before, and they would do it again.

But this was the first time they'd fought someone like Vic, and her sister would keep fighting for her until the end. Did that thief think those words would defeat her? Emilia steeled herself with her sister's words. Vic had been battered down while trying to protect everyone, including Emilia. Who would protect her sister?

Her soul drew into her. She gathered it from its depths. It was ragged and wispy, but it was hers, and this was her body. Amaya belonged in this cage, not Emilia. Amaya might have someone she loved, but Emilia did too, and she would fight here or die trying.

So she pushed against the wall, calling the last of her soul to fight against the barrier. She pushed with everything she had left, thinking of her sister. The times they'd laughed. The times Vic had pulled pranks and Emilia had defended her. The times Vic had stood up to their father and the bullies who had tried to hurt her. The day Vic had bonded with the scythe. The time Emilia had left Vic behind, choosing to be a vital.

Vic's eyes, hands, and laughter entered Emilia's soul. She could feel herself breaking, but she shoved against the wall. This was her sister—her loud, defiant sister—and Emilia was done watching her get beaten down.

"Stop!"

Emilia screamed over and over as her soul burned up around her. It didn't matter. This was her last chance at freedom.

Amaya thrashed and lobbed her soul at Emilia.

"This body's mine!" Years of taking other people's lives rushed through Emilia's mind, ripping at her soul.

"No. It was never yours to take!"

The wall thinned, then another woman stood before Emilia. Her edges were faded and ragged. The woman had thick red hair, and her eyes were black. She screamed at her.

"What are you doing? Why am I here?"

Emilia could feel herself fading, but she hammered at the wall.

"You've stolen enough lives, Amaya. You can't have my sister!"

The woman snarled, "Your life is the only one I'm taking. Why worry about her?" Amaya shoved Emilia away from the wall.

"Because she gives me strength." Emilia drew everything to her and slammed into the wall. It burst forward, and with a push of power, the woman screamed, fear in her eyes at finally facing death. In a blast, she evaporated.

Her body fell to the ground, and she tasted blood in her mouth. Emilia blinked. A glowing white energy surrounded her outside her body, and with a flicker of fear and anger, it faded to nothing.

Emilia touched her face. It wasn't an imaginary body in her mind. She held her hand out in front of her. It was covered in blood, but it was hers. A raspy giggle escaped her, but a pounding sound interrupted her.

"Love, are you all right?" Tristan asked through the door.

Emilia's victory was short-lived. She was in a bathroom, thankfully. "Yes!"

"Is it that soul? Are you okay?"

"Just a fight. I'll be fine. I'm going to clean up."

"It might be better that we find you another body after this is over," Tristan mumbled and walked away.

Emilia dug into her thoughts and didn't feel anything. She scanned the white bathroom to make sure the light was gone. Was Amaya dead? Gone forever? Had she just killed someone?

Her hands shook as she pushed herself up and started the water for a shower. She ducked under the hot spray. Her head felt light, and she could have slept for days, but it was time to put on the actual show. Would Tristan be able to tell?

She'd played the game for years, putting on a front to protect her family. As the water fell over her body, Emilia focused on Amaya's mannerisms and mimed them in the shower. She would watch and wait and bide her time. She had to believe her sister wouldn't give up. She would be ready. The originators would regret taking on the Glass sisters.

"**S**he's waking up."

She could smell something burnt as she opened her eyes. Bomrosy stood over her with a worried expression.

"Scared us for a minute there."

Vic tried to move, but pain flashed in her sides.

"Best not to move yet," Kai said from behind her.

She stopped. "Is Sam okay?"

"Yes. He wanted to go after them, but he actually listened when I asked him for help with you."

She lightly traced the bandages that covered her middle. "He stabbed me."

"You know he had no control."

Yes, she knew that Sam was abnormal when it came to radiant, but the fact that Tristan was always ahead of her beat into her mind. Was there any point in trying again? What if next time, Tristan ordered William to kill her again or hurt himself? Maybe she wasn't the right person to save her sister? After all, she kept messing it up. Vic shifted again and winced through the pain, but Kai steadied her.

"You shouldn't move," he scolded. He looked her over and let go when she leaned against the back of the sofa. "What's wrong?"

Vic laughed but stopped when that also caused her pain. "What isn't wrong? How long can we do this, Kai? It's just us?" She gestured to the room of five. "Do you think Tristan will set us up again? That was our last chance, and we blew it. He may be cocky, but I don't think he'll face us again with just William and my sister. It's over. We've lost. I'm sorry I can't help you with your family. I can't even save mine."

"This doesn't sound like you."

"Oh yeah, I'm supposed to keep going until I'm dead. Well, I'm sorry. I don't want to see Tristan's next trick. Maybe he'll make William stab my mother. Or maybe I'll get to watch my sister disappear."

Kai punched the edge of the sofa. "You saw it too. You saw her fighting. Are you going to abandon her?"

"Then tell me, Kai! Tell me the next grand plan? Why don't we gather up the reapers for one more death march, huh? Doesn't that sound good? Let's watch mogs and radiant slaughter them so I can save my sister. I can't ask that of them anymore. They lost their families too. But they've already realized what we should have long ago. We've lost. Get that through your head."

They stared at each other, then Kai lowered his head. "I get it. I'm frustrated too. Why don't we take a few days to recoup? Then we can think clearly."

Vic turned her head away from him. She was thinking clearly. Maybe clearer than ever. She could spare Emilia and William from watching her die. She refused to lose Kai and

Bomrosy, too. Someone had to put a stop to this, and it might as well be her.

Everyone moved around Kai's home in silence. No one wanted to speak. Still sore but the bandages working, Vic sat alone until darkness fell and the others went to sleep.

Scraps turned in a circle next to her and settled in, purring loudly. Vic stroked his fur and stared at the wall. She waited to feel sadness, anger, anything, but nothing came.

She bent over and kissed Scraps on the head, then took her scythe. Wincing, she stood and went to the door. Her vision blurred as she took in the small room, remembering when Kai had first brought her here. Beyond the faint burnt smell, she could still pick out cedar. The furniture was the same, but so much had changed. It might have been better if she'd lost to the mog that night as it had gripped her by the ankle. She wouldn't have had to live through losing her entire family.

Tears burning her eyes, she whispered, "I'm sorry."

With a click, she opened the door and locked it behind her before going out into the night.

❧

After leaving Kai's home, she wandered back down to Scrums Creek. The old apartment building she'd lived in to get away from her family sat empty. She spent a bit of time looking for the owner, but everything was dark. Who knew what had happened to him. He might even be a purified radiant now.

Kicking in the owner's door made a cloud of dust explode in the room and rats run for cover. She rustled around behind the desk, where he'd take payments, and found the set of keys to her old place. Vic propped up the door to the office, crossed the alley, and went up the stairs. The key stuck in the lock, but the door nudged open, and she shut it behind her. She tested the lights, but they stayed off. Looked like they still tracked gic, even at the end of the rebellion.

The sagging bed was still there. Vic sat down on it and stared at nothing until she passed out in an empty dream.

The days blended together, but it didn't matter to Vic. If she forgot to eat, she forgot there was no effort put into her living. She left and came back at night, locking the door behind her. Sometimes, she would find food, or on other nights, drain blight from imbs for food. She got nothing for blight since she no longer had a gauge, but draining imbs kept her in rice and maybe some fish. The freelancers had to risk everything to drain their gauges at charging stations.

Callum, the leader of the drain gang, changed the location nightly to avoid being caught by patrols. Vic hadn't even thought about how the banishment would affect freelance reapers. She covered her brand, but he knew she'd been part of an Order at one point. Vic could drain all night, and they got a cut of her food too.

There weren't as many patrols out here, and even in a rebellion, the poor were ignored unless they could be kidnapped to get purified. That was the biggest scare, apparently. Mogs no longer worried them as much.

Another night of draining done, Vic put her scythe away and took the food to Callum.

He sat in an abandoned building, sorting through packs with his gang behind him. Even though he was working, his lean body seemed to lounge as if he were taking visitors at a mansion, not a shack. With an angular jaw and dusky skin, he was attractive. Brushing long black hair out of his steel-gray eyes, he took the packs from her hands.

"Good pull tonight, Red."

Vic wanted to pull the hood tighter around her face but stopped herself. Part of her knew the nickname was to let her know he knew who she was, and he wouldn't tell anyone —for now.

"Know where you'll be tomorrow?"

He riffled through the food she'd brought and took out her share. Tonight, he generously gave her a few more packs of noodles. He set a bunch of carrots on top and tied them up.

Callum calculated a moment in his head. He was a planner and the type Vic would rather have on her side than against her. "Might stay around here another night. The factories cut down wages, so imbs are desperate to be drained." He put the food in her hands. "Why don't you think about joining us on a permanent basis? I'm not an awful boss, and we've stayed safe."

Vic shook her head, and he frowned. "It's better for you if I don't." She'd had people at her back before, and look where that had gotten them: purified, abandoned, dead. "Trust me."

A bit of steel showed in his gray eyes. "I can't take no forever."

The threat was clear when his gaze traveled to her scythe. Either he wanted it, or he wanted to make sure she was around so it could benefit them.

"Not today." Vic said nothing more. Helping them drain was only temporary. She would need to move on before she got them in trouble, too. Not that he was the best person in the world, but the imbs needed his services if they couldn't charge. The freelancers had already figured out that they didn't need to charge on their own. The things you find out when you can't afford to pay for it.

Leaving them behind after another night, Vic took a random trail back to her apartment. She took a different way each night to avoid being followed. So far, Callum hadn't tried anything.

Once home, she unloaded her food into the fridge. It wasn't cold, but it kept the rats and bugs away better than the cupboards.

How long could she go on like this? Vic sat on the ground and watched the sunrise through the window. The blight, a light green mixed with blue, taunted her with the colors of William's and Emilia's eyes. After trying to sleep and failing, Vic got up, covered her scythe and hair, and went out into the city.

She walked next to the canal, not paying attention to where she went. More people appeared the closer she got to the center of town by GicCorp. The statue before the gates stayed the same: an imb holding their wand to the sky.

Vic frowned, then froze before entering the town center. Around the statue and packed before the gate were radiant. They stood in lines, and people in the shops avoided looking at them as they worked, but Vic could see the fear in their hunched-over manner.

Rows and rows of radiant on the other side of the canal stood as a buffer before the corporation. What did Tristan and the body snatchers hope to accomplish? Use them as fodder if the reapers attacked again?

Her gaze paused on some imbs she recognized from the base, and she sobbed when she saw Kai's mother and sister staring blankly out into the shops. Did Kai know?

This was it. This was GicCorp showing its cards to the people of Verrin: cross us and you'll be one of them. There was no one left to fight for them. Tristan was showing the city that he'd won.

Her feet moved of their own accord, and she crossed the square to the bridge over the main canal. Vic pulled off her scarf and let the wind whip her hair free. The brand of two crossed scythes stood out on her pale neck. She took off the bulky shirt and dropped it to the ground. Her arms were bare in a black tank top, and she opened her scythe and planted the end on the ground.

It was stupid, and maybe no one would care, but Vic stood facing GicCorp and its forced army of radiant. No more fighting during the dark. No more setups by Tristan. If he wanted to take her down, she would stand here until he did. If he wanted to send his radiant army after her, she would knock them out until she died. The numbness broke apart inside her, letting her feel the rage from defeat after defeat.

Let him take her down in front of the city. He wasn't hiding his motives anymore, and neither would she.

She stood, and the people passing by her whispered and followed. Vic didn't respond to their questions. Her gaze stayed fixed on GicCorp. The sun beat down on her head, and her skin burned, but she didn't move.

When the sun reached noon, a figure appeared on the stone gate of GicCorp. Even from this distance, she could see it was Tristan.

He stood with her sister by his side.

His voice carried across the silent square. "You really want to be put out of your misery?"

Vic banged the end of her scythe on the stone. Her magic flared through her. "Come get me."

A low laugh came from him. "I don't have to. I just have to watch." He opened his palms. "Kill her."

In unison, the radiant stepped forward.

Vic closed her eyes and let the wind tease her hair. It wasn't a bad day to die.

"I can't let you go this easy, Sparks," a warm voice said from behind her.

"Kai? No!"

He grinned and gave her a cocky tilt of his head. "You aren't as alone as you think."

As the radiant approached, hundreds of people burst from the alleys. Vic opened her mouth as Julian led them to the canal. With a surge of power, they lowered their wands, and a stone wall shot up around all the radiant in the square. They tilted it inward so the radiant couldn't climb over as easily.

"How?"

Kai stood next to her. "While you disappeared, Bomrosy and I found everyone. Julian wasn't done helping us." Then from behind him, the remaining reapers gathered with Becks and Landon. "I told them we had one more fight in us. Don't we?"

"One more fight."

Imbs from the stores formed a wall so tall she could no longer see Tristan.

Julian marched up to her, and with the help of twenty imbs, they grew a ramp to the wall in front of Vic and the reapers.

She took her time walking up the ramp to stand on the edge of the new wall. A path formed in front of her as she kept approaching Tristan. Around him stood other originators. They all held their scythes. More paths formed over the wall as other reapers joined her march to the originators.

The radiant moved under them and tried to get at them, but they were too high up.

A few feet in front of Tristan, Vic clicked her tongue. "Shouldn't you do your own dirty work?" she taunted the body snatchers. "Here we are, the last of the reapers. There you are, in your stolen bodies with your old, crusty souls. Tell me, does it always end like this?"

"I'll let you guess how it ends every time."

"No thanks. I'll see for myself."

Tristan twirled his scythe in his hands. It moved like it was part of him. It made sense since he had thousands of years of working with it and control of magic that Vic couldn't even understand.

The reapers tensed, and Vic let a call rip from her. "To the end!"

A roar rose from the reapers as they charged at the originators. Magic burned hot through her scythe as she clashed with Tristan's weapon. Emilia stood behind him, watching.

The metal of their blades clanged and sparked as they slid them against each other. Vic swung her scythe at his neck, but he blocked it with a cut across his body.

The path she fought on widened, and she sidestepped to make more room for Kai, who faced off against Ethan. The other originator women fought, but Emilia held back. Maybe her sister was still in there.

Tristan swung at her right side, and she barely dodged back in time, almost falling off the wall. It kept the radiant out of the fight, but it wouldn't help the reapers who fell.

He laughed at her scramble. "Need help? Lover Boy, why don't you help me fight her?"

William climbed up the wall from the GicCorp side, and without trying to avoid her blade, he charged at her. Vic knocked out the back of his knees with the wooden staff of her scythe.

"You really can't face me by yourself, can you? What are you so afraid of, Tristan? I thought you wanted to destroy me." She opened her arms. "Here I am! Destroy me!"

"Watching you kill him will suit my purpose."

"Coward."

Tristan shrugged and stood back. William charged at her again, and Vic did her best to avoid him. Trying not to hurt him while he tried to kill her made it harder to fight. Her goal was to knock him out and save her energy for Tristan.

Her scythe burned with power, and Vic didn't know if there was something she could use against William.

He charged again and again while they danced on the ledge. The sounds of fighting surrounded them.

William stood once more, panting with a vague smile on his face, a knife gripped in his hand, the blade covered in dirt from her knocking him down. Vic could see her power swirling in the air. It was getting harder to hold back her magic as blight swarmed around her blade.

William stabbed at her side, and she used the flat end of

the blade to slap his hand. He dropped the knife. She kicked it away from him before he could pick it up.

Not caring about her scythe, William threw himself at her, knocking her down, the blade between them. Power flashed as it cut William's side, but he reached for her neck and closed his fingers around her throat.

Vic gasped for air. "Will, stop."

If William was in there, he didn't hear her. Dots of red and black encased her vision, and before she blacked out, she felt the surrounding power. Instead of burning white-hot, it moved like an ichor coated it , but Vic pushed it out from her scythe and blade. It hit William where his flesh met her scythe.

He flew back and convulsed on the ground. Dark veins popped up on his skin and faded repeatedly. His eyes burned red as his teeth gnashed.

She knelt by him and took his head in her hands. "What's going on?"

Tristan laughed. "You infected him with blight."

"No."

His body twisted and calmed, but the black veins crawled across his skin. She put her blade to him to drain the blight, but it wouldn't come out.

"That won't work. You don't know how to use your magic."

Vic clutched William to her and glared at Tristan. "Fix him."

Tristan chuckled. "What makes you think I'd do that?"

His blade came down in a flash and knocked Vic back. Pain flared through her arm, and blood splattered the ground. She fumbled for her scythe, but Tristan kicked her in the face. Her head swam as she rolled to the edge, radiant waiting below.

Tristan held the blade over his head. "I've seen this many times over the years. Somehow, it never gets old." The ancient eyes flashed, and he bared his teeth as he swung the point of the blade at her heart.

Vic kept her eyes open to meet her death, but in a flash of red hair, a body dove on top of her and took the hit through its chest.

Tristan's eyes went from triumph to horror in a matter of seconds. Vic rolled the body off her, only to see her sister impaled through the chest. Blood bubbled from her mouth as she tried to form words.

"What did you do?" Vic screamed at him.

For the first time, Tristan didn't smile. His face paled, and with a start, he ran down the wall toward GicCorp.

"Vic?" Emilia moved her mouth, gasping for air.

Vic put her hands over the wound. "It's okay. We'll get help." She scanned the battle as the reapers and originators fought on, ignoring the fallen around them. Kai was nowhere in sight, and William's skin was mottled with black blotches.

"Take m-my soul," Emilia gasped.

"What? I don't know how. Just hold on. We'll find someone. I'll get bandages." Warm blood bloomed around her hands, and Vic tried in vain to stop the bleeding.

"Listen." Emilia's voice grew firm. "You can take my soul. I can help him."

"No, we need to help you now."

"Sister."

Vic stopped looking for help and focused on her sister's eyes. The light green spoke of love and goodbyes.

"No. No. No. I can save you. I can." Helplessness encased her as warm blood leaked between her fingers.

Emilia reached out her blood-coated hand and stroked the side of Vic's face. "You need to know about the magic."

"Em?"

"I could see in her soul, too. There's no magic, sister. Blight is human souls. The m-magic are souls they've kept here and corrupted. Y-you need to send them t-to the After, where they belong."

"What?" Vic's mind raced as she tried to help her sister.

"There's no blight. Only souls. Souls can shape the world. Now take mine and h-help him."

Tears streamed down Vic's face. "No, I can't lose you. I can't. Please, we can fix your body."

"Gather my soul. Y-you can do this. You're so strong. I love you." Emilia's eyes faded.

"I'm supposed to save you!"

Her sister smiled. "No, remember? I-I was saving you." Emilia took a shaky breath, and her eyes went blank, a smile resting on her face. As Vic held on to her scythe, she saw the bright, clear light of her sister's soul leaving the body.

Sobbing, Vic let her scythe take in her sister's soul. "I love you too." The soul connected to the scythe, and Vic sensed her sister. Everything that she was, the love she felt for her, and what she wanted Vic to do.

William's body had turned entirely black when Vic cut his skin with her blade. She let her sister's soul go and pushed it into William.

In moments, he stopped convulsing, and his skin took on his normal tan. He breathed easier, but he didn't wake up.

The battle clashed around her as she sat with her sister's

body. Her gaze went to the path Tristan had taken. She knew where he'd gone. Vic gripped her scythe. Her body tense, she ran into GicCorp. He wouldn't live for another hour.

❦ 25 ❦
TRISTAN

His wife was dying, and no one would help. Tristan held her clammy hand in his. She was growing weaker by the minute. Her crimson locks had turned dull and brittle. The green eyes no longer had laughter in them, but blankness. Delicate lips that used to kiss his shriveled before his eyes. Reapers were supposed to have power, but he didn't have any to stop his wife from slipping away in a traitorous body.

With a rattling breath, Amaya blinked her eyes open, and for a moment, life flickered in them when she met his gaze.

He leaned forward with a lukewarm bowl of broth and held it to her lips. She took a sip but turned her head away, drinking no more.

"One more, love? Can you just drink a bit more?"

She didn't have the energy to smile fully, but she took one more sip to please him.

"You need rest, too," she whispered weakly.

He pulled the blankets around her. "Don't worry about me. Just focus on getting better."

Her eyes held the truth about that statement, but she didn't reply. There was no point. They both knew she wouldn't get better.

A light knock on the front door interrupted them, and Tristan finished smoothing the blankets. "Rest now. I won't be far."

He went out of the bedroom they shared and softly shut the door behind him. The home was modest, but it was theirs. The wooden floors and walls used to glow with the care they gave them. In the weeks after Amaya had fallen ill, Tristan hadn't focused on cleaning, only her care.

He opened the front door, and Conrad lifted a brow at his state. Then he pulled Tristan into a hug. "You aren't eating."

Tristan patted his friend on the back. "I'm eating enough. Are you just here to talk about food, or did you look into my idea?" Conrad had been there for him throughout Amaya's sickness; he'd sat up with him many nights, listening to her shaky breathing with him.

"Can I come in?"

Tristan stepped aside and gestured to the chairs in the kitchen. "Would you like a drink?"

Conrad glanced at the stack of dirty dishes. "No, thank you."

He sat across from his old friend. "Well?"

"It's no use telling you it's forbidden to take out souls from the living."

Tristan leaned in and put his palms on the smooth wood of the table. "But it can be done."

Conrad pulled a worn book from his jacket. "Yes, it has been done before. I stole this from Morgan's private collection. It took some work to even get in." Conrad handed the delicate book to Tristan. "Taking a soul has a price, but you have to be able to hold it. That also has a cost."

The pages were thin in his hand as he looked through the book while Conrad waited. "Using souls?" Tristan looked up. "They have this kind of power?" This whole time, he'd been letting that power slip through his fingers. They could have been harnessing souls to bend anything on Earth.

Conrad held up a hand. "Keep reading."

It grew late into the night as the two flipped through the pages. Tristan leaned back in his chair and rubbed his hands through his messy hair. "If we tie the souls to us, they become corrupted and will try to infect other bodies. Reapers are immune, but humans aren't. But we can harness the power from our scythes to give humans the power to form as though with magic."

"But it isn't magic. It's souls."

Tristan eyed the drawings of the monsters in the book. Too many souls would try to find another body if they weren't released into the After. They would attach, fight over the body, and transmogrify into something that would eat humans. The souls would never stop hunting until they were freed.

"We could make something that blocks the souls from entering." Tristan's mind spun. They could live in a world where things were formed. The possibilities would be endless.

Conrad tapped the book. "And I think you're missing something."

Tristan quirked his head.

"If we put your wife's soul into another body, it would have to fight it. We would have to make something to trap or remove the soul."

They'd made barriers before. Their magic protected their souls against a corrupted soul that didn't want to leave. "We could make one inside the body?"

"Possibly. This also means we could live on."

"Live on?"

Conrad pushed back his chair and stood. "We could keep living. Forever."

Tristan heard a soft cough from the bedroom and stood. He teetered on the edge. Was he willing to destroy lives to keep his wife forever?

A hand rested on his shoulder. "Think on it. We would need a few of us to agree since it would require many scythes to hold millions of souls. But we spent our lives protecting and moving souls to the After. Isn't it our turn to benefit?"

Tristan clasped the book in his hand, and Conrad left him in his house with his thoughts. Another cough came from the room, and he rushed to his wife's side.

With a cloth, he dabbed away the blood from her mouth, and she smiled. "Who was that?"

Tristan brushed her hair away from her sweaty forehead. "Hope, my love. Hope."

❧ 26 ❧
VIC

The power drew her into the center of GicCorp. Red power pulsed, but many of the scythes were missing. Tristan knelt next to the containers with the white light, muttering to himself crazily.

Vic clanged her scythe's blade on the floor, and he jumped to his feet, rage twisting his face.

"You took her from me!"

The normally calm, cocky man looked ragged.

It was Vic's turn to let him hear a sarcastic laugh. "There was nothing to take. You don't belong here, and whoever that was in my sister's body didn't belong here either."

He took his scythe with both hands and tried to hack at Vic. In his anger, his attack was sloppy, and Vic blocked it, shoving him back. He faltered and continued to glare.

"Her name is Amaya. She's my wife!"

Vic took a deep breath, and her ribs expanded as she shouted, "She's my sister! What gave you the right to pick your wife's life over all the others you've destroyed? The blight are souls? What did you do?"

Tristan sneered. "Reapers moved souls on for years. We deserved a reward. My reward was that my wife got the plague? I had the power to stop it, and I did. Souls can create and bend things at their will." He flung his arms out. "Without souls, you'd have nothing!"

Vic pointed her blade at him. "I'd rather have nothing than corrupt souls to make my house. They don't belong here."

A vein popped in his forehead. "What do you know about anything? You don't even know what you're supposed to do or how to do it. Leave the city to us. We created it. It's ours to do with as we please."

Vic crossed over one of the metal lines that led to the glass containers. "You think you have a right over human life? You think you can do as you please? I don't know what to do? Even I can tell you didn't do your one job! You're supposed to help souls to the After, whatever that is, not keep them here to live out your immortal fantasy with your wife."

At the mention of his wife, Tristan's face pulsed with pain, and his lips twisted. He took two containers out from the power source. "This is your mother and father. Would you put them in a body to let them live or send them on?"

Vic's chest burned as she looked at the souls Tristan held. Her eyes blurred. "Where are their bodies?"

"Gone. The body rots without a soul. Your father was one of us and my closest friend. Don't you want him to live? He helped me create this!"

She blinked and tried to keep breathing. "He changed. He knew it was time to move on. My mother wouldn't want to stay at the expense of another life."

Tristan narrowed his eyes and threw the glass down. It

shattered, letting the souls out. More pain crossed his face as he looked at the glowing souls. They twisted together. Vic reached out her hand, and the souls caressed her as if saying goodbye. A single tear tracked down her cheek.

"Aren't you so righteous?" Tristan sneered.

His scythe had knocked her to the side before she could react. Her body, already wounded, flinched as more blood leaked from her side.

Vic skimmed her blade across his staff. As their scythes clanged together, they heated.

The power of the souls swirled around them, and Tristan laughed. "You can't control them."

Power burst from him, and in a staggering blow, Vic flew through the air. Tristan spun his scythe as the souls bent around him. It was never air that he used, but the blighted souls.

She gritted her teeth and drew them to her, but it felt heavy and wrong. The souls screamed in pain, then like piercing an old wound, she let her scythe release them and launched them to freedom. They blasted through and created a hole in the ceiling to the sky.

Blood dripped from her nose.

Tristan screeched, "What are you doing?"

"Letting them go. They aren't ours to use. Can't you feel their pain?" The blight swirled around her as they squared off.

"They're mine. They are in the orbs. They are the city. They only go when I say they can go."

"Not today." Vic drew more to her, and the air whipped around her as she let them go, crumbling the ceiling further.

Tristan's blade sliced her across the shoulder. Before he could attack again, Vic jammed her scythe's staff into his middle and cut him with her blade. Blood spilled onto his neat clothing.

He was fighting with too much anger, and his movements were sporadic. Tristan plowed forward, and with each blow, he spoke, "Give. Me. Back. My. Wife."

Vic's arms shuddered as she blocked his hits. "You thought my sister was weak. Well, it's your wife who lost."

A roar echoed in the air, and he lunged at her. Vic ducked and cut into his middle. He toppled over, his scythe flying out of his hand. Vic kicked him in his wound, turning him onto his back.

Blood caked his face, but it wasn't really his face. The only true part of Tristan was the soul coming through the old eyes. "You would have done the same to save your sister. You think you're better than me?"

"I know I am." With a final swing from her blade, she cut through him, burying the point in the ground.

The burning scythe flared with the screaming voices of the thousands trapped in the city. Her scythe called out to the corrupted and abused souls that had been kept down here with no way to escape.

Vic didn't know what to do, but she let the power of the reapers flow into her blade, and a beam of light pierced the top of the building. It flamed white-hot, and the blight rushed into her scythe from the air and Verrin's very foundation. The walls of stone crumbled around her as she released the souls the city had been built on.

The rest of the ceiling collapsed, letting her see the sky. The swirls of blight collided into the beam of light and surged away to a peacefulness that Vic assumed was the After.

The souls screamed their relief as they passed through.

Vic held on to her scythe as it burned her hands with raw power. She reached out to the souls that didn't belong here. They were too old and out of their time. One by one, she grabbed them and forced them along with the blight. Bodies dropped to the ground. Vic could feel them all.

Strings of power burst as she called the radiant souls. She let the souls enter the radiant to free them, then they too moved on. The radiant woke up, and Vic could feel everything.

It could have been hours or days, but then one last soul remained. It fluttered to her and stroked her cheek before it said goodbye. Tears fell again as the soul flew away.

In the crumbling stone, Vic collapsed. Only rubble was left of the city, and water flooded into the place where GicCorp had once stood. She held on to her scythe and didn't bother to get up as the water came. On her back, she blinked as the brilliant blue sky, clear of blight, blinked down at her. Vic's lips turned up, and she closed her eyes.

27

WILLIAM

Nightmare after nightmare flew across William's mind. Not only had he tried to kill Vic, but he'd tried twice. He'd thrown his soul at the wall for days, but it didn't matter. He was a spectator in his own body.

Now, ragged souls beat at his wall, and he didn't mind if they took him. At least he would never harm anyone again. They flashed in different colors, and only a few showed any humanity. With claws, they wore down the wall he couldn't even manage to push through.

He sat and watched. After all the fighting and trying to help Vic, he knew this was the best way to save her. He let it happen as the wall ripped aside, and he waited for the first blow, but it never came.

He opened one eye, only to see that the creatures were gone, but a woman stood next to him, glowing. Green eyes close to her sister's looked down, and she put out a hand for him to grab.

"Emilia?"

She nodded. "You met me before." Her soft voice calmed

him, and she looked around William's cage. "Not too long ago, I was trapped, too." With a wave of her hand, she took down the remnants of the wall.

"How are you here?"

"I asked Vic to put me in here to save you." Her face was drawn. "My body's beyond repair, and it was my time to go."

William rushed around the room, or maybe it was his mind. It wasn't clear to him where he was. "No, we can put you back and heal you! Vic needs you. She fought so hard to save you. You can't give up."

Her hand stopped him. "Moving on when you're supposed to isn't giving up." She blinked a few times. "It's okay to feel angry and sad about death. I have to admit, I'm scared to move on and leave her behind." Emilia took his hand. "But I know you'll look out for her. She needs someone to lean on, even though she won't admit it. My sister's strong, but even she needs help from time to time. With the city falling, moral leaders are needed more than ever."

"Can't you stay too?"

"I wish I could." She let go of his hand and folded them in front of her. "If I stay, I'll have to take over another body, and reaper power was never meant to be used this way."

"Reaper power?"

"While I was stuck inside my body, I could see into a woman named Amaya. She was dying when her husband broke the rules the reapers followed. They took souls to power their immortality and this city. The wands and rings were all laced with reaper power mixed with souls." Emilia twisted her hands together. "From what I gathered, the more they used the souls, the more damaged the souls became. They called the damaged souls blight." She looked off, as if seeing something he couldn't. "My sister's letting all the souls go home now." Emilia looked more like light than herself.

"Where are you going? I have so many questions."

"I know, but it's time for me to say goodbye. There's a book on how they learned the magic, but I would recommend destroying it. Goodbye, William, and thank you for being there for my sister. Let her know I was happy to save her, and I'd do it all over again." Emilia blinked and smiled softly. "I love her so much."

"I'll tell her."

In a swish of light, Emilia disappeared from his mind. With a groan, William opened his eyes. Dust clouds floated in the air, and the stone wall had collapsed under him. He got to his feet as water rushed in from the canal. Bodies covered the ground. William went to the first one, and they were dead, as if they'd fallen over with nothing left inside.

William froze at the sight of a body with the same color of hair as him, lying face down in the water. He stumbled over other bodies to get to it. Shouts moved around him, and tears streamed down his face as he reached for the shoulder and turned the body over. His heart thudded in his ears, and he let out a choked gasp of pain when the body's blank brown eyes looked up at him. It wasn't his brother. Sadness and relief flooded him. He stumbled up and searched through the bodies being taken away in the overflowing canal.

"Sam!" William frantically sloshed through the water. "Sam!"

Some in GicCorp radiant clothing ran toward higher ground as the stone disappeared around them. From the rubble, William saw a thatch of hair that matched his own.

"Samuel?"

The head turned, but there was no vacant smile. His brother blinked and ran to him.

"William!"

The two brothers embraced, and moisture pricked William's eyes. "I thought I'd lost you."

"I've always been here, Brother."

William squeezed his brother, not wanting to let go. He felt shame over how he'd treated Sam and gratitude that his brother was finally free.

"I'm so sorry, Sam."

His brother slapped his back. "I'm equally pissed and proud of you, Brother." He let him go, and his eyes were so full of life that William wanted to keep looking at them.

They climbed over bodies, checking for anyone who was alive before the water rose.

"Where's Vic?"

Sam pointed to the beam of light that shone in the sky. The swirling colors of blight were sucked into the light, leaving behind a blue sky in its wake.

The brothers paused and looked up at the sky in the light of the brilliant sun not covered by any blight.

Sam put his arm around William. "You found a girl that gave us the sky."

What color is the sky, Brother? "I did. Let's find her before she does something foolish, like sacrifice herself for the city."

"It'll take a lot for you to keep up with a fire girl."

William smiled at his brother, and they ran to the fading walls of GicCorp as more water flooded in. Next to the stack of scythes, Vic lay in a pool of water, her red hair floating around her and her scythe clutched in her hand.

He bent over her, and she was breathing. He sighed with relief and lifted her from the water. "Grab the scythe and whatever else there is, and let's get out of here."

All that remained were a few scythes and book covered with a worn cloth. Sam took everything and followed William out while he carried Vic.

Kai, Bomrosy, and Xiona stood at the top, directing people toward radiant land. That was the only place where buildings still stood. He met Xiona's eyes, and she bowed her head. Guilt ate at him over all those he'd purified.

His brother nudged him. "You can feel bad later. We need to find a place for the injured."

The healers still wore their blue uniforms as they set up in various radiant homes. There were no more imbued bandages to heal people quickly, so they had to revert to old techniques. William put Vic down, and a healer rushed over to look at the long cut down her arm that still leaked blood. She wasted no time in cleaning out the wound.

William stood back and watched her work.

The healer looked at him. "You can go get another."

Not wanting to leave but knowing he was of little use standing over them, he and his brother went to help. They gathered bodies for burning and helped build a wall to keep the water out. The imbs kept trying to use their wands and were confused when they didn't work anymore.

Radiant helped those who no longer had magic. A group of people went out to the fields to gather what food they could before the water flooded everything.

They worked into the night. There was no light but fire, and in the darkness, they tried to manage. They built big bonfires by felling trees with rusted tools.

William checked on Vic often, and she still slept. After a

few days, he moved her into his house. His mother and father helped build temporary walls to keep the water out.

Various people and leaders were chosen among them, and they met to decide what to do. The city was sinking, and they couldn't hold back the water without magic, so they would build boats and try for the land Ivy and Freddie had told everyone about.

After a long day, William sat by Vic. Her head was hot, and he worried that without magic, an infection would win. He spent his days packing supplies and building boats.

No mogs rose from the water anymore, and even though everyone was tired and dirty, a strange peace had settled in Verrin. The huts where the radiant lived would soon be under water too, and in the next few days, they would move out.

Sam slid down next to him. "You know, if you work yourself to death, you won't get to see her again."

William rubbed his thumb against her skin. "It's hard to see her like this."

The brothers sat next to each other, both tired from the day's work.

"Sam?"

"Yeah?"

"I'm sorry." William ran his hand through his hair and looked into his brother's eyes. "I'm so sorry. I should have listened to you. The radiant were wrong, and I've purified so many. I've ruined so many lives." Sobs racked his body.

His brother gently shook his shoulder. "You did what you thought was best. I won't say purifying them was right, but you gave us a better chance than becoming a mog. If anyone's to blame, it's the body snatchers for creating a world that needed people to be purified. They're responsible for all those deaths. Not you."

"It's nice of you to say," William muttered. "But it doesn't make me feel less like a murderer."

Sam sighed. "That's up to you, Brother. You can live in guilt or look at all those you saved because they got another year. But I don't think Vic sees you as a murderer, and I don't see you that way either."

William pulled the blanket over her body. "I hope so."

Sam nudged him. "If you feel so bad, you can spend the rest of your life making up for it by helping others. Who knows what we'll find on the other side of this swamp? It can't be worse."

William reached into his pocket and pulled out the paper boat Sam had made and handed it to him. "Maybe we can put that in the water when we reach our new home?"

"Definitely." Sam tucked it in his pocket. "And someone will need to teach my future sister-in-law how to make them."

They looked down at Vic's still form.

William brushed aside her hair. "Wake up, Vic. You did it. You can wake up now. We still need you." Even though his body ached for sleep, he sat back, holding her hand and hoping she would open her green eyes.

❦ 28 ❦
VIC

Everything hurt, and Vic thought she was dead. But if she was dead, would she feel so much pain? She squinted her eyes open and saw a rough wooden roof. She turned her head. William was asleep next to her, slumped against the wall. Her movement woke him, and he opened his eyes and leaned toward her.

"We didn't think you'd ever wake up!" His hands brushed through her hair, and he looked in her eyes, as if making sure she was real.

"Will?" she croaked and lifted her hand to his face. "It's you?"

He took her hand in his and nodded. "Yes. I'm myself again."

Vic didn't want to even blink as he put another pillow under her to help her sit up. "Where are we?"

"My old home. Radiant homes and items are the only things that survived the loss of magic. The stone practically vaporized in most of the buildings, which is good since no one was crushed. But the city is flooded in areas, and we don't have many handmade boats."

As William rambled on, Vic smiled. "It's nice hearing you talk."

He grinned sheepishly. "Yeah, Sam's even worse."

"Sam's okay?"

"Same as he used to be." William smiled, but it was filled with sadness.

Vic grimaced as she pushed off her blanket. "Are you feeling guilty about it?" She hit him lightly. "I doubt he's still mad at you, so let it go."

William reached his arms out to help her stand. "You shouldn't be walking."

"No, I need to get up." Vic leaned on him and tried not to wince. He helped her to the door, and she looked out at what was left of Verrin. A short wall divided the swamp from the land, and she heard hammering as hundreds of people worked on boats in an empty field.

"We're leaving?"

"We have to. The city is sinking. We should have enough boats in the next few days to transport everyone. At least there's still a lot of fish since most of the fields flooded, and after picking the fruit we needed, we had wood for more boats."

Vic took in the smaller version of Verrin. People were packed around makeshift tents, doing various tasks of cutting or shaping wood. Boats floated in the water outside the low wall. Hundreds of boats.

"The leaders are meeting tonight, and I'm glad you're up since I wanted to show you something first."

"Becks, Bomrosy, Kai, his family, Maddox—"

William held up his hand. "Maddox is fine."

Vic breathed a sigh of relief.

"Everyone made it. Even Xiona."

"She's—"

"She will face a trial when we get to land. For now, she's doing hard labor like the rest of us."

William took her around the radiant land before making her go back to lie down. Then he got out a case with cloth in it. She raised her brows, and he gestured for her to open it.

Inside was an old book. Vic had never seen one this old. The paper was thin but well preserved. The writing was difficult to read, but from the pictures, it had to do with reaper powers.

"Is this an instruction book?" Vic leaned in to read it better.

"More or less. It explains how scythes let souls go to the After, but it also mentions what the power of souls can do and how to keep them here."

They exchanged a look. "We need to destroy it."

William nodded. "After we tell the others. It also explains how you're supposed to pass on souls that get stuck. The first-generation scythes were supposed to be the only scythes. The ones from the originators were passed on to the reapers. The other generation scythes don't work anymore."

"How did they decide who got one?"

William bit his lip. "There aren't that many reapers left. Only thirty-three, counting you. There are more scythes than reapers."

She touched the brand on her neck. They were almost wiped out. "Did we really win? Is this winning?"

He took her hand. "I don't think anyone wins in a war."

"So, we're leaving Verrin." Vic wasn't sure how to feel. Tristan had taken her entire family. They wouldn't get to see the unknown land or struggle to build something together again. Her sister had given everything up for Vic, and she wished it could have been the other way around.

William squeezed her hand and gave her a knowing look. "The Glass sisters are stubborn and always trying to save each other. She was free at the end, Vic. She loves you very much."

"I know. I wish I'd had enough power to save her."

He brushed the pages of the book. "You do, but you didn't. That's what set you apart from Tristan."

Her fingers caressed the pages, and she wondered what had gone through Tristan's mind as he'd sacrificed others to save the woman he loved. Vic didn't want to, but she understood him, and maybe she was a bit like him. Emilia had saved her by not letting Vic make that choice. Her sister had moved on, unwilling to corrupt souls to save herself.

"I'm a lot like him."

William took her face in his hands and brushed his lips against hers. "No, you aren't. And even if you think that, you have too many people around you who would stop you, out of love."

"Ah, Sally Sunshine thinks he could stop me?" Vic brushed a strand of hair away from his forehead.

His eyes warmed as he looked at her. "If anything, I could just sit on you. That would give the others a few minutes to help me out."

Laughter burst from her mouth as she cried, sad over everything that had been taken, but hopeful for a different future. She pulled his face down to hers and kissed him, letting their shared pain intermingle, but finding a flame of happiness together.

THE BOATS WERE READY, AND THEY WOULD LEAVE WITHIN THE hour. Vic called the reapers to meet where the former wall had surrounded the city. She waded through the swamp and found a narrow stone platform to build a fire on, and smoke rose against the blue sky she'd never tire of looking at. It was early morning, and so far, the only colors happened at sunrise and sunset. William stood next to her, and she held the book in her hands.

The reapers approached, and they'd gone back to wearing their standard black. Kai stood closest to her. His half grin gave her confidence. Becks and Landon nodded to her. Vic looked over the battle-worn reapers and pushed her shoulders back.

"I know we have a lot to prepare, but I needed a moment of your time. This is something that concerns only us, the reapers."

They gathered closer, and Vic took out the book. "Behind the scythes, there was a book about how the reapers' powers work to move souls to the After. There's also the forbidden, which allows reapers to move their souls into other bodies and create wands and rings. To corrupt the power."

The reapers muttered among themselves.

"My sister said to destroy it." Vic's voice trembled slightly. "I hope you all agree with her. We fought to end GicCorp, and I hope reapers will never become that again."

Becks crossed her arms. "I agree. We keep the part about how to use our powers, but I don't plan on ever doing what they did."

"There's a time to live and to die. We are very familiar

with that and what happens when we go against nature. If I never have to kill a mog again, I'll die happy," Kai responded.

The rest of the reapers nodded. "Burn it."

Vic carefully pulled out the pages about the After and handed them to Kai. The rest she threw on the flames. The pages curled and turned to ash. Vic looked out at the reapers as they stood witness to the end of what Tristan and her father had created.

"This will only be enough if we pass on our stories of what happens when we cheat death. We need to tell future reapers about what we lost to be free of blight and the originators. This is for my family. My father, mother, and sister died because of this."

William took her hand. The reapers echoed the names of all those they had lost, honoring them in the hovering smoke. Hundreds of reapers down to thirty-three. They would fight to keep the memories alive and make sure something like this never happened again with human souls.

One by one, they left. Plans were made to cross the swamp to a new world that waited for them. For once, there was hope.

Vic walked hand in hand with William to their boat. What was left of their lives was packed in a small bundle, which Scraps had made into his bed. They each took a paddle and pushed off under the blue sky. Sam's boat was next to theirs, and Maddox waved to Vic as they went ahead. Kai winked at her as he lifted his sister into another boat. Becks shouted orders as the boats left behind the sinking city. No more walls, mogs, or charging orbs. The last people of Verrin headed out into the unknown.

Their boat floated over the land that used to be the Glass house, the glass having collapsed like the stone, but in her pocket, something had survived: the glass figure of a cat. Vic pictured her sister's mouth as it would twist up while she created something new. Warmth spread through her hand as she held the figure. They paused, and Vic smiled her thanks at William. Vic gently touched the water, and the ripples spanned out and reflected the cloudless sky.

"Goodbye."

Her family hadn't seen the world without blight, but Vic could almost hear them in her heart.

She turned to William. "Let's go?"

He squeezed her hand, then followed the other boats. There was no way to know what was out there, but they would face it like they'd faced everything else: together.

THANK YOU

If you found any enjoyment from this book please consider leaving a review. For every review I get, a puppy gets snuggles.

But in all seriousness, thank you!

Also, if you want to keep up to date on releases and get some free short stories: Sign up for my newsletter!

https://www.subscribepage.com/maridietzauthor

ALSO BY MARI DIETZ

ACKNOWLEDGEMENTS

I never imagined how hard it would be to finish this book. I reworked it and worked on other things, but even though this last year was tough, I knew I had to finish their story.

Life didn't go as planned, and this book ended up being late. Thank you, readers, for your understanding and support. I hope this last year hasn't beaten you up too much, and I want you all to know I was right there with you.

I don't think this book would have happened without my video calls. In a world where we were shut out, I still got to talk to my support system.

The Women Warriors and Fire Hazards, you listened to my struggles with this book and stood with me while I tried to write. With your strength and belief in me, I was able to finish it.

I want to thank my wonderful beta readers, Nicollee, Sarah, Helen, Angela, and my mom. Without you, I wouldn't have found some of those mistakes. Thank you for your comments and especially your time. It means so much to me that you took the time to read this and give me feedback.

Also, to my awesome editor, Elizabeth. I say this all the time, but you give me the confidence to publish my work. Your help makes me better, and I'm so thankful for you!

Many thanks to Ravenborn for her beautiful covers. They make Vic come to life for me, and this one with the blue is just gorgeous.

And thank you, Stacy Rourke, the blurb doctor, for helping me write my blurbs. They always come together so nice, and it takes so much stress away when you help me.

Last of all, thank you, readers. Thank you for coming to Verrin with me. I hope you join me again in my next adventures. The greatest joy I get is to share my stories with you.

This is only the beginning.

ABOUT THE AUTHOR

Mari Dietz wrote her first poem about crickets when she didn't even know how to write. Her mom typed it up for her on an old typewriter. From then on, she was a goner to the written word. Over the years, she fell in love with the world of fantasy and thought maybe one day she could write something too.

She took a few side roads and got a major in Theater and English. Then she somehow ended up teaching in South Korea for three years. Now back in the middle of nowhere, she teaches Creative Writing and writes her own books in her "spare time," when not distracted by lesson plans, anime, or K-dramas.

Four rescue dogs give her the privilege of living with them, and they keep her sane-ish.

This is her debut novel and series. If you want to contact Mari, feel free to connect on:

Twitter
Facebook
FacebookGroup
Website
Amazon
Instagram
She can't wait to hear from you!

facebook.com/maridietzauthor

twitter.com/marildietz

instagram.com/maridietz